MIDLIFE MAGIC AND MALARKEY

A PARANORMAL WOMEN'S FICTION NOVEL

COUGARS AND CAULDRONS

JENNIFER L. HART

ELEMENTS UNLEASHED

*For my Aunt Marion Kiley-Wilcken,
Who wrote to me, called me, and kept me informed. And
didn't let MS get the best of her. I will miss you.*

MIDLIFE MAGIC AND MALARKEY
COUGARS AND CAULDRONS BOOK 4

Midlife Magic and Malarkey
Hart, Jennifer L.
Print ISBN: 9798851432484

A killer by any other name is just as deadly....
Samantha Sinclair has taken charge of refurbishing the bed and breakfast on the Outer Banks. Even though Multiple Sclerosis limits her physically, everyone in the community of aging witches and shifters believes Sam is doing a fabulous job renovating the place, especially Mathis and Damien. It's no surprise when a secret admirer leaves little love tokens for her. Sam is sure the gifts are coming from one of her shifter mates. Until a body washes up on shore with another message written in blood.
Can Sam and her cougars stop the supernatural stalker before he strikes again?
Midlife Magic and Malarkey is the fourth installment in

the Cougars and Cauldrons paranormal women's fiction series. If you like strong female characters, steamy romance, and heart-pounding adventure, you don't want to miss Jennifer L. Hart's enchanting tale. Buy *Midlife Magic and Malarkey* and weave a spell today!

Midlife Magic and Malarkey

CHAPTER 1

SAM

The rage of a middle-aged woman is like a tube of toothpaste that some jackass squeezed from the middle. It erupts out into the world in a gooey mess but there's plenty left inside for another go.

"What do you mean the fridge won't be delivered until next Monday?" I barked into the phone at the customer service operator unfortunate enough to pick up my call. "This is the third delay in a month. What am I supposed to do with my brie? Row out to an iceberg and chip a chunk off?"

"Ma'am," the clueless young buck began, and I growled in response. Adding a ma'am to the situation never helped anyone in customer service. Ever. Because the ma'am in question knew it was a substitute for *listen up, you difficult bitch*.

"I want to speak with your supervisor," I snapped. It might have been my imagination, but I thought he expelled a sigh. Probably relieved he didn't have to wrangle the unhinged customer anymore.

"Easy, little witch," Mathis Dracos had come up behind where I sat at the check in desk and began massaging my neck. "You don't need to verbally castrate this one, too."

I glared over my shoulder at him. He flashed me a brilliant smile, probably thinking that would somehow save him from my wrath. Or Wrath as I'd dubbed the writhing emotion that had taken up residence in my chest after my last doctor's appointment. It was an entity that lived in my body but was a separate being from Samantha Sinclair.

I covered the mouthpiece and hissed, "Aren't you supposed to be painting the shutters?"

"Done. What else do you have for me?" The tone was suggestive. Mathis, once you got past the grim and imposing exterior, was a giant flirt. At least with me, though I'd seen him make Damien blush a time or two.

Unfortunately for him, I wasn't in the mood for witty banter. I wanted the freaking refrigerator I'd painstakingly picked out three months ago. The whine of a saw carried down from the second floor and I waited for it to subside before speaking, "Call Jerry and find out what the hell the deal is with those countertops. We can't finish the bathroom until the stone remnants are delivered."

"I'll do it on one condition," Mathis knelt beside my chair so that we were eye to eye. "You'll take a break after this. Damien's bringing dinner from *Second Chances,* and we want to spend time with you."

It was bribery and blackmail all rolled into one. I knew for a fact that he would make the call. He also wouldn't tell me where on the green Earth my stone remnants were until I agreed to the break. But that was how Mathis operated, the sneaky, underhanded wretch.

I couldn't possibly love him more.

"It's a good thing you're so pretty. You'd be hosed if you had to get by on your charm," I informed him.

"Is that a yes?" He flashed me a grin, knowing he had won.

I sighed. "Fine. An hour for dinner."

"Don't you have a chat with John tonight?" He raised a brow.

"No, that's Wednesday."

His dark eyes assessed me. "It is, Wednesday, Sam."

"It can't be." I whirled around to face the computer. "What the hell happened to Tuesday?"

"You spent it having a fit because the ramp leading up to the peach cottage was too narrow."

I opened my mouth to retort that I didn't have a fit, but that would be a lie. As a shifter, Mathis could smell a falsehood. As my familiar, he knew how I was feeling, the same way I knew how he and Damien felt most of the time. They each took up a spot in my brain that I was gradually getting used to being aware of, though the idea of privacy had gone the way of the dodo.

I looked into his dark eyes and let out a slow breath. "I have been a bit of a bitch, haven't I?"

He would never say it. He didn't need to. I knew the truth.

"You've been stressed." He gripped my cold fingers in his warm calloused ones and brought my knuckles to his lips. "We miss you."

Damn, he knew how to play me. Even without a mystical familiar link I knew both Mathis and Damien were concerned about my health. Burning it at both ends was par for the course for a woman in her twenties. But I was fast approaching my fifty-second birthday and had the extra wrinkle of multiple sclerosis to complicate matters. I needed to be smarter than this if I wanted to keep from being bedridden by the grand opening.

"There she is." Mathis winked and took the phone from my hand where the easy jazz music still echoed. "Tell you what. You head home while I finish this call and find out about the stone, okay?"

"Because you're a big damn hero?" I raised a brow.

He pretended to buff his nails on his denim work shirt. "Why else?"

Because if I got back on the phone and another middleman who didn't know his ass from a hole in the ground told me the refrigerator that I'd ordered months ago was delayed again, my head might explode.

I pressed my lips to his whiskered cheek and then reached for my walking stick. "Okay. Make sure you—"

He kissed me, effectively cutting off what would have been another demand. When he pulled back, I was breathless.

"I got this," Mathis murmured and swatted me gently on the butt. "Go get ready for dinner."

I couldn't keep the smile off my face as I headed out the door to where my Jeep was parked. The three of us had officially moved into Damien's trailer when the contractor told us that all the plumbing and electrical at the B&B had to be updated for the renovation to continue. It had put us behind schedule for several weeks. The demon I knew only as the Investor who owned the place had been breathing down my neck. Since he decided that he was in fact a he— choosing a gender was something demons only did after they'd been on the mortal plane for several months—he'd turned into a micromanaging dick.

"It takes however long it takes," he'd said on our last Zoom conference. "I trust that you're overseeing every detail."

I had been. Still, it felt like some sort of personal failing on my part that the renovation wasn't farther along. Would I have enough time to complete it?

No, I couldn't think like that. As a witch, I knew the power of belief as well as the threefold law. I'd been putting a lot of angry words out into the universe over the past several months. Was it any wonder I was losing days and had more holes in my memory?

The drive to Damien's trailer— he kept insisting it was ours but he'd lived there first so I always defaulted to thinking of it as his— only took a few minutes. Just down the highway and then over the sand so I could park in front of the place. My corgis, Wally and Wilma, greeted me with zoomies as they raced from the bedroom to the living room, into the kitchen, and back again. I clipped their leashes to their collars and took them down the ramp for walkies.

After they'd done their business, I headed inside and dumped food in their bowls before making my way to the shower. My silver-streaked brown curls were wild with humidity and I felt grubby, as though the dust from the renovation had settled in my every pore.

I fiddled with the water temperature, the middle-aged version of Goldilocks who lived in fear of being too hot or too cold. Either would drain my energy reserves down to nothing. I'd miss both dinner and my chat with my son and maybe even my grandbaby.

John and Jessica had moved out of this very trailer a few weeks after their daughter had been born. The decision had been Jessica's but John supported her, not just because she was the mother of his child. Weird things happened around the fifty-and-up community for aging witches and shifters that I now called home. Supernatural things. This wasn't a place for a young family with an infant.

I was halfway through shampooing my hair when the bathroom door opened. Damien poked his head in. Unlike Mathis, Damien was my age, though he wore the years a hell of a lot better than I did. His body was fit and toned, which was usual for a shifter even one in middle age. The only true signs of time were the deep laugh lines around his eyes and mouth along with the distinguished silver at the temples. His blue eyes lit up when he spotted me.

"Mathis said he'd get you home for dinner. Bribery or blackmail?"

He too, knew the evil twin's methods. "A little of column A and a little of column B. Though I'm not sure if the guilt trip was him or me."

"Want me to wash your hair?" His expression turned

hungry with the prospect. Damien loved to play lady's maid for me.

"Just my hair," I warned him. "No funny business. I'm hungry and John's calling in an hour."

If either of the shifters got me into bed they had a habit of keeping me there, to rest as well as other things.

He feigned affront. "*Moi?* Funny business? You must be thinking of your other mate."

He stripped down. Even though I was the one to make the call that there would be no sex I still admired the view. My shifters had it going on. Plus, I was tired, not dead.

"Turn around," Damien said.

With one hand on the *oh shit* bar to keep my balance, I did. I also began to sing. *When Doves Cry* had blared from the workmen's radio during their lunch break. The song was stuck in my head so that was the tune I chose. Both Damien and Mathis loved it when I sang and I found myself doing it more often just because the experience seemed to relax them both. Plus the shower had really great acoustics.

Once I deemed myself clean and Damien had rinsed my hair and combed through it with his shifted cougar claws, I reached for a towel. "Why is it that I can never say the right thing to get you to relax, yet the second I sing, you're like putty in my hands?"

The towel paused where he'd been drying my tresses. "Firecracker, I am *anything* but putty when you sing."

I yelped when he pressed a very not malleable part of his anatomy against my damp backside.

"You know what I mean," I huffed and tried to pull

away from him. He didn't release me though he did step back and put more distance between us before he continued towel-drying my hair.

"It isn't just us, Sam," Damien paused as he moved the towel lower to swipe at the droplets that had run down my back. "Your voice is incredible. Ethereal. Everyone who hears you sing is moved by the experience. And you said you never studied?"

I shook my head. "Mom never wanted me to join any of the musical programs at school."

The towel paused again. "You never talk about your mother."

"What's there to say?" I shrugged. "She died when I was nineteen. Before my brother Ray got sick."

Damien took a dry towel and wrapped it around me to absorb the last of the water. "And you father?"

"Never knew him." I shrugged, feeling more exposed than I usually did being naked with one of my shifters. Nudity wasn't a big deal to either of them, though I wasn't so sanguine about prancing around in my birthday suit. For one thing, I was nowhere near as fit as either of them. I still hadn't gotten up the courage to join in with the naked dancing under the full moon that the coven did. MS was my excuse for not participating, but the being naked part was what I truly avoided. Some habits were just ingrained too deeply.

"So, what's on the menu?" I forced a bright tone.

Damien's blue gaze assessed me. "Angel hair pasta with homemade pesto and rosemary olive oil bread sound good?"

"Sounds like a carb fest. Where do I sign?"

Damien threw on a pair of athletic pants while I poked through my closet trying to focus on what to wear instead of ghosts from my past.

Some thoughts should stay buried.

Dinner was part of the Damien Moss culinary experience, aka a slice of heaven. I'd just set my napkin aside when my phone rang with the video call chime.

"Take it outside, you two," Mathis ordered in a playful tone. "I don't want to hear about the baby's bowel movements for fifteen minutes."

I cast him a withering look, but the phone was still ringing. Damien snagged it and my walking stick, holding the phone up so I could see Jessica and John, along with my precious granddaughter Emily crammed together on the screen.

"Hello, my little loves." I grinned at the three of them. "Bear with me a moment, we've been banished from the house."

John's blue eyes, the mirror image of his father's, narrowed. "Tell Mathis I'm going to kick his—"

"John," Jessica's voice held a warning note.

"Butt," John finished, looking as though the word didn't satisfy him at all. I knew it didn't since he got his potty mouth from me.

"You can try, punk." Mathis hollered. I let the screen door slam a little hard because I could feel his satisfaction radiating through the familiar bond. Mathis felt weird about our family dynamic, like he didn't have an official role. He stuck to what he was best at, being a heckler who gave grief. Sort of a belligerent uncle who could also shift into a cougar and tear out an enemy's throat.

Once I was settled in the wicker loveseat, Damien scooted in beside me so he could appear on camera.

"You guys need a better setup," John groused. "Dad, half your face is cut off. I'll send you specs on a decent laptop and camera."

I rolled my eyes even as Damien said, "Son, we're Gen-X. All we need to get by is coffee and sarcasm."

Everyone laughed and the feeling that radiated from Damien was like the first rays of sun warming the sand. It was so nice to see him content after everything he'd been through.

We'd lost his mother a little over six months ago. Though I swear I could still see bits of my friend Alba Moss in my granddaughter's eyes. Only Damien and I knew that Alba had worked a magic spell to protect her great-granddaughter—as well as the rest of us—from a disastrous bargain. And in the end, her soul had been reborn into a family that loved her.

We chatted about their week before the baby began to fuss. "I'd better get this little one off to bed." Jessica used her hand to make Emily wave a pudgy fist. "Say bye-bye to Gram and Gramps."

"Night night grandma's little pumpkin." I made kissy faces and then watched as Jessica lifted her and carried her into the next room.

"So, Mom, how are renovations going?" John asked.

"Don't get her started," Damien grumbled.

I nudged him hard in the side. "Ignore him. And renovations are coming along. I think the grand opening will happen on time. Are you guys still coming for it?"

"We wouldn't miss it," John grinned. "Bea's been pretty insistent that we should visit."

"She was just up there last month," I complained. Unlike me, Jessica's grandmother could leave the convergence where mystical ley lines crossed. My healing magic had been born in this place. I didn't know what would happen to me if I tried to use it anywhere else but since Alba had told Damien that I couldn't leave without my power destroying me, we had all decided not to risk it.

So, I had to wait for my son and granddaughter to come to me. Which sucked. Patience may be a virtue, but it wasn't one of mine.

John signed off shortly after and Damien and I sat together and stared out over the ocean. The late April breeze made white caps tip the waves. I shivered.

"You okay, firecracker?" Damien put his arm around my shoulder and buried his nose in my hair.

"Yeah," I spoke absently, my gaze fixed on the Atlantic. I loved this place. Loved my life here with Damien and Mathis. But damn it, would I have come back here so soon knowing I was checking into an East Coast version of Hotel California? Sure, I could check out any time I liked, but I could never leave.

"Liar." Mathis stood at the screen door, shamelessly eavesdropping.

I scowled at him. "It's not nice to call your mate a liar."

One sardonic brow went up. "And is it nice to lie to your mate?"

He had a point.

"I'm just feeling a little...I don't know how to describe it. "Overworked. And penned in." I shrugged. Multiple Sclerosis had limited my world by sapping my energy and taking things like a smooth gait away. Basic stuff took more than I had some days. There was so much I wanted out of life still. But I was without the means to procure any of it.

"Restless," Mathis supplied as he pushed his way out onto the porch. "You feel restless."

I considered it and then nodded. "Yeah. I guess that's part of it."

"What can we do to help?" Damien soothingly petted my hair.

If there was anything they could do to cure me, to take away all the anger that churned like the waves out there, I would have told them. I would. But there was no enemy to fight. My body was the battleground, the disease the creeping foe. And as awesome and understanding as they both were, neither of them was great at dealing with problems that had no fix.

"You guys do enough," I turned and smiled up into his blue eyes. Damien had his restaurant to run, I didn't want him taking time off to babysit me. "This is just something I need to work through. Even if it means I must chew on contractors and customer service people a few times a day to take the edge off." I pushed up from the chair and leaned heavily on my cane. "I'm tired. Think I'll turn in early."

I could feel the disappointment coming through the mate bond. From both of them. They were men. They wanted to make it better. It was their fatal flaw because sometimes there was no solution.

Sometimes the world kinda sucked and all you could do was deal.

CHAPTER 2

SAM

I was seated at the check-in desk in the B&B going over the latest estimates for the attic windows when I heard the car pull up. All the construction workers were on their lunch break and Mathis and his twin brother had gone over to *Second Chances* to help Damien by serving a catered lunch for the chamber of commerce. I wasn't expecting anyone and welcomed the distraction. Windows were both expensive and boring.

"Careful on the stairs," I called out at the sound of footsteps thudding on the fresh boards. The contractor hadn't put the railing in yet and the last thing I needed was for the UPS guy to fall face-first into the bushes and sue us.

The screen door creaked open and I was glad I had just put Wally and Wilma out back in the small fenced-in area so I didn't have to worry about attack corgis. We were expecting several deliveries. The new light fixtures I'd bought from eBay, new matching flatware that would replace Alba's impractical silver hodgepodge. The linens with the B&B's new name, *the Sawgrass*, on them for the suites, but those weren't due until the following week.

The delivery person who came through the door wasn't dressed in the little brown shorts. Instead, they wore a white sheath dress that seemed much too revealing for the April morning.

"Mel, aren't you cold?" I greeted the true shifter. Mel could change into anyone at any time. Their typical form was a five-foot-seven bombshell with white-blond hair that was shorn up the back and violet eyes.

"Nah," Mel shook their head. "Shifters run hot and true shifters hotter than most."

Damien and Mathis ran hot, too, at least compared to me and my poor circulation. Then my gaze caught on the item they held. "What's with the flowers?"

Mel set the overlarge vase on the counter beside me. "These were delivered to the bar earlier. The note says they're for you."

I frowned as I studied the arrangement. It was a huge extravagance, a dozen red roses nestled in with baby's breath. The card was printed by the florist. I turned it over and saw my name typed out along with the words, *love, your secret admirer.*

"That's weird," I frowned. "Why would Damien or Mathis send these to the bar and not here? Or to the trailer? And what's this secret admirer nonsense?"

Mel shrugged a slim shoulder. "The delivery dude looked a little lost. If they said *the Sawgrass* B&B, he might not have known where that was."

"Well thank you for bringing them over," I said. "I could have come to get them."

"Honestly? I was hoping to get a look around. I haven't been here since Alba...."

Since Alba died. I nodded. "Well, let me give you the grand tour."

We started in the parlor just to the right of the main hall. Under Alba, it had been a sitting room, but I'd decided to swap it out for the dining room. That way the sitting area overlooked the sound at the back of the house and the dining room was closer to the kitchen.

"The floors look great," Mel said. "Bamboo?"

I nodded. "Yeah, they're really scratch resistant and much more sustainable than hardwood. It breaks my heart to think of chopping down trees for us to walk on."

Having a level surface throughout the B&B was one of my primary concerns, along with widening the doorways and installing ramps and safety rails to keep the place handicap accessible.

"This looks fantastic, Sam." Mel spun through the sitting room area with their arms spread out. "So much more light this way. And the bay window seat adds a ton of charm."

The gas fireplace had been installed the week before. It was getting too late in the season for a fire, but I admired the little faux diamond stones so much that I'd been putting it on first thing in the morning as a little ritual.

"What kind of furniture are you thinking of putting in here?" Mel asked. "The space is so light it would be a shame to weigh it down with those heavy antiques of Alba's."

I agreed. "Anything John or Damien wanted to keep,

they've already taken. The rest is in the storage unit outside. I was going to invite the community in to take their pick before donating the lot."

"You could sell it," Mel suggested. "I'm sure some of it is valuable."

It was. The problem was I didn't have enough spoons to deal with photographing and listing every single piece in Alba's extended collection. Damien and John didn't have the time. So donation it would be. "I think Alba would want these things to benefit someone in need."

Mel smiled but it didn't reach her eyes.

I put out a hand. "You okay?"

They nodded. "Yeah. I just…I really miss her. She was such a fixture here, you know? Every Tuesday night in the winter she'd come to the bar and she, Ginny, Javier, and I would play poker. Alba won nine times out of ten. I used to accuse her of using her foresight to cheat."

I snorted. "Like she would have to resort to that."

Mel sighed and leaned against the stained doorframe. "So do you think you'd like to join our poker night?"

"I'm horrible at cards." Leaning on my cane I used my free hand to wave at my face. "Everyone can easily tell if I have a good hand or a lousy one with a single glance."

Mel grinned. "Okay, it was just a thought. We don't see much of you lately."

There was a question in the true shifter's eyes. Was I avoiding them? I hobbled back to the front desk, taking a moment to figure out how to answer without giving anything away. "I know. I haven't managed to make any coven meetings either. I feel completely off-kilter these days. Coming here to deal with whatever fresh hell awaits is about all I'm up for."

I swallowed and looked out the front door. It was too cool yet for the full-on tourist season. Soon the beach would be crowded with travelers. The heat would sap my energy still further. I hated thinking about how much all that would drain me down until I had nothing left to give.

I hated that it seemed like no matter what direction I turned I was letting someone down.

Mel covered my hand with one of theirs. "Sam, it's okay. We all know you're doing what you think is right. For Alba's memory and the community. And obviously, someone appreciates it." They gestured to the ridiculous roses.

"I'm gonna kill those two," I said. "Flowers are such a waste of resources."

"Can I give you a piece of advice?" Mel asked.

I raised a brow. "Could I stop you?"

"Probably not." When I looked up into their eyes, they continued, "Just appreciate the gesture and shut the hell up about it."

A crack of laughter escaped. "That ungrateful, am I?"

"No, not ungrateful at all." Mel smiled to soften the harsh words. "I think you get really focused on practical shit and forget that life is meant to be enjoyed. What happens if the grand opening had to get pushed back for a week? Or a month? No one will die, right?"

"Well, I certainly hope not," though I'd been striving for a light tone, the words fell flat.

"Look, I don't mean to butt in. If cards aren't your thing, that's cool. Come to the bar and sing. Get together with the coven and celebrate the full moon. Clothing optional. Or here's a thought, do nothing and lie out in the hammock for a spell."

"That sounds nice," I closed my eyes and imagined it. "Really nice."

"All that and more can be yours for the low low price of saying I'm all out of fucks to give. People don't come live in a place like this because they're type-A workaholics, Sam. Now I'll shut up and go check out the rest before I offend you."

"You can't offend a friend." I winked and watched them head upstairs. My gaze strayed back to the roses just as the phone rang.

"Sam?" My GC asked.

The tone immediately put me on edge. "Rip it off quick, like a band-aid."

"We failed an inspection."

"What?" There went my good mood and all thoughts of lounging in a hammock. One of those things no one tells you about having a beachfront business. The getaway that the tourists all enjoy isn't part of your day-to-day. I needed to hustle. *The Sawgrass* was Alba's legacy and it was left in my fumbling hands.

Letting out a sigh I pulled up a new document. "Tell me what I need to do."

DAMEN SPOTTED Mel the second the true shifter walked into his kitchen. The food was done and Mathis was busy monitoring the tables out front. "How did it go?"

Mel hopped up on his prep table and picked a piece of grilled chicken off the plate. That piece had been too charred to be served to his guests, so Damien had set it aside for his own lunch. "I did my best. The flowers were a nice touch, by the way."

"Flowers?" Damien's brows drew down. "What flowers?"

Mel shrugged. "A dozen red roses."

Damien shook his head. "Sam says flowers are a waste of resources."

Mel rolled their eyes heavenwards. "See, women *say* things like that and yet they still appreciate the gesture. Thankfully Mathis is less literal than you."

"Hey, I listen to my mate." Damien turned to the sink and began attacking the dishes with a vengeance. "Sam hates waste. She says it's a four-letter word and I happen to agree."

"Yeah, yeah. And the place looks beautiful. But is it worth the price?"

No, Damien thought. He and Mathis had been trying to get Sam to take it easy, to back off the renovation details, or at the very least delegate some of them. But Sam had become a witch on a mission.

Mel moved from the prep counter and picked up a towel. "You know anyone in the community would be happy to help you guys out at any time with anything. We all owe you and Sam our lives."

"I know that," Damien snapped.

Mel dried a sauté pan and then sent him a sideways glance. "She hasn't called a coven meeting since John left."

Damien nodded.

Sam was the leader of both the coven and the shifter pack. Two roles she seemed to want to forget she'd inherited. But meetings and rituals were important to their community. It bonded them together through the difficult times.

Mel watched him carefully. "You need to talk to her. The patrols need to be re-established."

"Everything's been quiet," Damien argued.

"Too quiet." Mel gave him another speaking glance. "The calm before the storm, Damien."

He slammed the metal container he'd been scrubbing into the sink. "Damn it, Mel, don't you think I know that? What would you have me do?"

"Talk to your mate," Mel hissed. "Make her understand."

Damien turned away. "I've tried. Mathis has tried. Ginny has tried. She's driven by a whip and none of us can see who or what is wielding it."

"She's a witch and an honorary Alpha," Mel said. "She needs to learn to delegate."

Damien nodded. "She takes our suggestions as a criticism though. Even the Investor doesn't expect the level of commitment that Sam is putting into the place."

"Talk to your mate." Mel wrapped their fingers around his arm. "Help her to see before she wears herself down to a nub. We're all concerned about her."

He swallowed and nodded. "I'll try again."

Mel left and Damien went back to clearing up the kitchen. Normally he liked to go out and greet the members of the Chamber of Commerce. But he wasn't in the mood to deal with humans.

Mathis came in carrying two trays heaped with dirty dishes. His gaze roved over Damien's face. "What's wrong?"

"Sam." Briefly, Damien told him about sending Mel in as an emissary.

"And let me guess, she said all the right things and went back to what she was doing with no promises made?" Mathis asked.

It was uncanny. Mathis had known their mate for a fraction of the time that Damien had but the other shifter understood her so much better. That chafed Damien's pride and he snapped, "Well, the flowers didn't work either."

"You bought her flowers?" Mathis scowled. "Sam doesn't like flowers. She says they're a waste of resources."

Damien stared at him for a long moment. "I thought you sent them."

"Where would I get the money? I work for your miserly ass, remember?"

All the hairs had risen along the back of Damien's neck as their gazes locked.

"Maybe it was John?" Mathis suggested.

"Maybe." Damien didn't believe it. A dozen red roses was a lover's gift, not from a son.

"I'll ask around when we get back," Mathis said. "Call the florist."

Damien nodded. "Eric can finish up here. Go now. I've got a bad feeling Mel's right."

"Right about what?" Mathis asked as he tugged off his apron and tossed it on the counter.

"The calm before the storm." Damien dialed Sam's number, needing to hear her voice. "I'll keep her on the phone until you get there."

Mathis was out the door in a flash. Sam picked up on the third ring. "Damien? What's up?"

"Just wanted to hear your voice." Not a lie, just not the whole truth. "So I hear you have a secret admirer?"

Her laughter warmed all the shadowy places in his heart, and he decided not to tell her about his growing unease. Mathis would be there to protect her soon. He didn't want her worried until they knew for certain there was a reason to be concerned.

Hurry Mathis.

CHAPTER 3

SAM

Make time to rest or MS will make it for you. It was something I understood very well and felt deep in my marrow. The bevy of phone calls had gone on all afternoon and by the time Mathis had arrived, I'd been so flustered that I was practically levitating.

"There's nothing you can do here, little witch," he assured me.

I put my head in my hands. "How could this happen? I was sure we had put in enough smoke detectors. The GC told me we had."

"Let me take you home," Mathis urged.

I shook my head. "No, there's more—"

He got in my face. "There's always more, Sam. It will all still be here tomorrow. You slept like shit last night. Let me take you home, give you a massage and you can get some rest."

That sounded nice. Too nice. "I don't think—"

He cut me off. "Or I can tie you to the bed. Your choice."

"You're not the boss of me, evil twin." I snarled.

He snarled back, "Whoever is has been doing a lousy job so as your mate I'm staging a mutiny on your behalf."

Stubborn pride would have made me fight, but that was just a useless way to burn up energy bucks I didn't have to spare. "Fine."

"Fine," he growled back. "I'll go get your dogs."

I watched him head into the back room and turned to face the computer. Smoke detectors. Of all the stupid things to miss. I still had to write an email to update the Investor. Even the easy going demon wouldn't be happy at yet another delay. Hopefully, this wouldn't put us too far behind.

I typed out a quick update and had just powered down the computer when Mathis returned with my corgis at his heels. He didn't need the leashes. The dogs obeyed the shifters with unspoken commands but being so close to the road made me nervous. Mathis knew that so he clipped the leashes to their collars and then rose.

I sensed his uneasiness through the familiar bond. He was prepared for another round of talk sense into the stubborn witch.

My gaze fell on the flowers for a long moment and when I looked back at him I let all of my frustration go. "Thank you."

He blinked. "What for?"

I rose, leaning on the walking stick he'd carved for me. "For taking better care of me than I do of myself. For fighting me for me. In a lot of ways I am my own worst enemy."

He swallowed and then held out his hand for my keys. I gave them over without a fuss.

Fifteen minutes later I was snuggled up in bed while Mathis massaged my neck and shoulders. He'd pulled the curtains so the early afternoon sunlight was blocked out. The room was cool and dark. Wally and Wilma snored from their fluffy, doughnut-shaped dog beds.

We hadn't spoken since we'd come in. I could still feel his frustration through the bond. I could also feel his satisfaction. Much like Damien loved to bathe me, Mathis reveled in being able to soothe my aches and pains with his touch.

He was so restful to be with. Never asking for more than I had to give, including my thoughts or voice. The man who called BS when I told even a white lie preferred total silence to pretty platitudes. I didn't deserve him. Or Damien either. Or the coven I was letting down by avoiding the gatherings.

I was a witch, a healer. De facto alpha of the shifter pack. So why did I feel like such a liability?

Mathis dug into a particularly stubborn knot, and I flinched. "Sorry," he breathed.

"It's okay."

The mattress dipped as he sank beside me, his hands moving closer to my spine. "Is it really, Sam?"

I turned so I could look him in the eye. "No, it really isn't. I know I'm pushing for too much too fast. I know you're worried about me, but I can't seem to stop."

"We can't help if you don't let us in," he breathed. "I

can feel your overwhelm. The frustration and exhaustion that's hanging around you like a dark cloud. But I don't know how to make it better for you."

How to explain my fears? "I guess in a way I feel like *the Sawgrass* is my penance."

"Penance?" Mathis frowned. "What for?"

I let out a deep breath I hadn't realized I'd been holding. "I fucked up. A lot. By keeping John from Damien. By staying with Robert for too long. By not saving Alba—"

"Not your fault," Mathis growled.

"It feels like it is. She was the heart and soul of this community. And everyone's looking to me to be some sort of leader. But the truth is, it's easier to stress about tile and lose my shit over deadlines than to disappoint all of you."

Sensing my distress, Wally and Wilma leapt up onto the bed, offering solace in the form of a cuddle.

"Sam." Mathis cupped my cheek. "No one is disappointed in you."

I shrugged. "I don't know what I'm doing."

"You think I do? You think Damien does?" He pursed his lips and then shook his head. "Never mind. Damien is his own creature. If he doesn't know what he's doing, he fakes it like a boss."

I snorted.

Mathis shooed the dogs off the bed and climbed in behind me, pulling me against his warmth. I breathed in his scent, jalapenos, and heat. "I haven't got a clue, little witch. Not about anything. I've operated on instinct my entire life. And for most of it, it was just Eric that I had to look out for. But he has Ginny now. So you're getting all the worry and nagging I used to heap at his feet."

"I don't mind," I murmured and snuggled deeper into his warmth with a yawn. "I know you're just looking out for me."

"Get some sleep, little witch." He kissed the top of my head.

I drifted off with a smile on my face.

Mathis waited until Sam had fallen asleep to head outside. Eric stood there in cougar aspect.

"Did you get a scent from the flowers?" he asked.

His brother shifted and reached for a beach towel that Mathis had draped over the railing earlier to cover his nudity. "No. The only scent on the vase was Mel's. I called the florist. They don't have any men working there. The owner wouldn't tell me anything about the guy who bought the flowers. I think I was giving off a jealous ex vibe."

Mathis swore and ran a hand through his hair. "I don't like this. Sam is already stressed. I don't want to keep things from her but my instinct is screaming something's not right."

Eric leaned against the porch railing. "What can I do?"

Mathis shook his head. "Nothing. Damien and I need to talk this over with her." Disquiet settled low in his belly. Could this be someone from her past looking to rekindle a love affair?

The thought made his nails lengthen and sharpen into the cougar's claws.

"I know that look. Go for a run, brother. I'll watch over Sam until Damien gets home."

Mathis shook his head. "I don't want to leave her. Go home to your wife."

Eric grinned and clapped him on the shoulder. "Don't have to tell me twice. Are we still meeting up at *Mel's* for dinner?"

When Mathis nodded Eric dropped the towel and shifted back. Despite his worry, he smiled seeing his twin so full of life.

It had all been worth it, the pain and suffering from their pasts had earned them this reward. This sweet life. Sure, it had its ups and downs, but he had a mate to hold every night and a lover who helped him protect her. Mathis stared out at the endless expanse of rolling waves. The railing was rough beneath his palms. He wanted to go back to the bedroom and hold his curvy little witch, feel her softness. Something held him in place, his gaze fixed on the churning water.

He thought of Sam's words. Penance. That explained the feelings of guilt that he and Damien had picked up on. She'd tried to stuff it down, to ignore it. They knew she missed John and Emily. That she hated being contained in the convergence and that she mourned Alba. But penance? It made no sense.

Not that anything that went on with his little witch made much sense. The depth of her feelings were as endless and temperamental as the sea. It was how she had room in her heart for both him and Damien. And it was a good thing because being mated to Sam was more than any one shifter could handle.

His phone rang and he answered without looking at the number. "She's sleeping."

"Any leads on the flowers?" Damien asked.

"Nothing. Whoever delivered them must be Sam's secret admirer."

"Hang on." The sound of sizzling filled the background and Mathis could easily picture Damien standing over a frying pan working his magic with his cell cradled between his shoulder and ear.

"There might be another possibility we haven't considered," Damien said when he came back on the line. "What if the flowers were from the demon?"

Mathis snarled at the thought of one of those heinous beings making a move on his witch. It was one thing for the Investor to own the B&B, another entirely for him to be sniffing around their mate.

"I feel the same way." Damien breathed. "But we should ask him before we upset Sam's applecart. She's going through enough stress."

"She claimed *the Sawgrass* is her penance." Mathis didn't feel at all guilty revealing her confession to Damien. He knew if she had spoken her piece to her other mate that Damien would tell him. It was understood that there wasn't room for secret confidences in their unorthodox relationship.

Damien blew out a breath. "There's no talking her

out of that, is there? Does this mean she won't relax until the place is up and running?"

"If then," Mathis growled. "Damien, I don't think we can wait for her to work this out on her own."

"Do you have any suggestions?"

"I threatened to tie her to the bed."

A low chuckle filled his ear. "Oh man, and she didn't shred you on the spot?"

His lips curled at the memory "She got a little snarly. Nothing I couldn't handle."

"I'm sorry I missed that." The background noise from the restaurant faded out and then Damien said, "I'll be home around eleven. You'll take care of her?"

"Always," Mathis said.

"You know what I mean." Damien sighed. "She needs release."

Mathis was surprised. "Why didn't you say anything last night?"

"I was hoping that maybe she would want us to ease her. She's always so melancholy after she talks to John though it seemed better to let her sleep."

"You don't want us to wait for you?" It wasn't something they'd discussed but always it

had been the three of them, together when things turned sexual. It was a show of trust that Damien was urging him to comfort Sam on his own.

"Not this time," Damien breathed. "I think it's better if she doesn't think we're ganging up on her. So this one time I'll take the demon, you get the girl."

Mathis laughed softly. "We'll be thinking about you the whole time."

"You're such a fucking liar," Damien snarled and disconnected.

Mathis headed back into the trailer. He'd gotten the better end of the bargain. But still, he felt almost...nervous.

Damien had always been there to hold him back in case anything was too much for Sam. The fact that Damien had enough faith in him gave Mathis the courage to approach his witch.

Sam had rolled onto her back in sleep. Her plump lips were parted, and behind her closed lids, her eyes darted back and forth. Mathis was about to pull the sheet away and reveal her body when the first tear tracked from the corner of her eye.

Sam

"Ssshh, baby. I've got you." The warm liquid smoke voice wrapped around me like an embrace, pulling me out of my restless nightmare. *The cold sterility of the doctor's office, the phony sympathy on his face. There's nothing more we can do. You'll have to adjust as best you can.*"

I sniffled and pressed deeper into the warm solid mass of my shifter's chest, breathing in his hot spicy scent. Letting it calm me.

"Want to talk about it?" Mathis murmured in that low way of his.

I shook my head, keeping my face buried. "I never remember my dreams." Not a lie, because this was a memory.

There was a pause. "I'm under orders to pleasure you?" He said it like a question.

"Under orders?" I glanced up into his dark eyes. "Who would dare?"

He didn't speak but his expression clearly said, *who do you think?*

Damien, of course. And in his way, by "ordering" Mathis to service me like I was a mid-sized sedan needing an oil and filter change, gave Damien the ultimate control, even when he wasn't here. The wretch. I should refuse, just to spite him.

As though reading my thoughts, Mathis murmured, "You can always say no."

I knew that. I also knew that no matter what he threatened, Mathis would never tie me to the bed, not even if I begged him. Well, maybe if I begged him. But I wouldn't. Our mate bond told me that while he wanted free access to my body, Mathis had no desire to play power games with me. He wanted a lover, an equal. Someone who could and would say no if things went too far.

"How do you want me?" I asked instead.

"Anyway, I can get you." His thumb glided over my lips a moment before he pressed the most tender kiss there.

Just FYI, this is gonna get graphic. I plan to enjoy

myself with my sinister lover. If reading about that isn't your thing, skip to the next chapter. We'll meet you there.

After we let off some steam.

I was already naked so my focus went on getting him into the same condition. By the time he'd shucked his boots, yanked off his socks, and pulled his shirt over his head my nipples ached for his mouth. I loved having the familiar bond open while we made love. I felt a hot, potent desire from him. It made mine flare like adding gasoline to a campfire.

Mathis unbuttoned his jeans gifting me with a tantalizing glimpse of his goody trail. I licked my lips as I watched him push the fabric down his legs until he stood naked before me. Stalking like the predator he was he crawled back onto the mattress, dark eyes hungry before he rolled on top of me for another searing kiss. His hand slid between our bodies. His fingers stroked over my folds, parting me to tease even more wetness from my core. I bucked into his calloused hand and reveled in the feel of him there. Needing to feel him deeper, I parted my thighs.

This I still had. This I savored even as the fear whispered, *it might end. You could never feel this way again.*

No. We'd barely been together for six months. I wasn't ready to give up on this part of my life, or this connection. Not yet. Shoving all those worries aside, I focused on his heat, his scent, all the good things that made Mathis who he was.

"Please," I whispered, arching into his touch. My body had grown slick and ready for him.

I expected him to guide himself inside me. Instead, he pulled me close and then rolled until he lay flat on his back with me sprawled on top of him.

"Like this?" A spike of apprehension went through me. Being on top wasn't my favorite position. Gravity was a bitch to aging breasts. Being exposed that way had always made me feel self-conscious. And when I was worried about that, I had a hard time finishing. And then there was MS, the numbness, my balance issues...too many things could go wrong.

His lids were heavy as his hands traveled up my sides until he could cup my breasts. "I've imagined this a thousand times."

My heart softened. When he said things like that how could I refuse?

I sat back, staring down at one of the men I loved. Mathis was a gift that I never would have imagined for myself. Having two incredible males in my bed...there were times I felt like the greediest witch on earth to have them both. I let all of that flow through our bond as I took him in hand. Slowly, careful to position him at my entrance, I guided him into my slick passage.

He shuddered beneath me as I slipped slowly down his length. Loving the hard press of his flesh within. The way his gaze locked on that spot where our bodies were joined and traveled up over my softly rounded belly, to my breasts that he still held, then to my face.

"More," he grated. His hands trailing down to my hips, as though to guide me. "Take me deeper."

I lifted my hips, sliding back off of him, and then plunged. Again. And again.

And that was hunger that radiated through our bond. Need so sharp that the feel of it had me clenching around him. Mathis threw his head back and bucked up under me. At that moment I understood why women enjoyed this position. Mastering a lover, riding him to completion. Heady stuff. Worth the risk.

He bucked hard beneath me, throwing my weight forward. I went with it. Planted my palms on either side of his head and used the leverage to writhe on him. My breasts bobbed in his face. He cupped them again in his rough palms, kneading the flesh, working those taut peaks until they throbbed. His lips closed around one as he bucked up into me. He laved and sucked until I cried out, then he switched to the other side, even as his fingers continued tormenting the first. It was my turn to throw my head back, reveling in the sensation of hot, wicked fulfillment.

The hard plunge of his cock, the heat of his mouth, the tug of his fingers, the worship in his eyes. It was amazing. But still not enough.

"Mathis," I groaned as frustration clawed at me. "I can't come. Not like this."

He released my breast and then guided me off him. "Hands and knees, little witch. I'm going to fuck you deep."

My whole body quivered in anticipation as I got into position. That wasn't enough for him though. Mathis dragged me to the edge of the mattress, so he could plant one foot on the floor for leverage. I felt the prick of the cougar's claws at my hips and the rough caress of his textured tongue up my spine. I shivered in response.

When he surged inside my body my lips parted on a silent scream. Relief coursed through me. That was what I needed. Words spilled from me. I wasn't even aware of what I said. Only the feel of his hands gripping my hips and the hard drive of his thick shaft in me.

"So good," he panted and circled his hips, lighting me up from the inside out.

"Yes," I gasped in agreement.

His right hand slid down and around searching through my curls until he found my clit. He rubbed it, fast and quick, spreading more of my need around the sensitive bud until I grew delirious from the pleasure. "Oh yes, right there."

In my ear, his liquid smoke voice rasped, "Come for your mate."

Over. I shattered, clamping down hard on him, holding him inside me. He pumped once, twice, and on the third thrust bellowed out his release. It went on and on for ages, eons. Stars were born and died in that endless expanse of time.

Still semierect within me, Mathis pulled me back down onto the bed. His claws had retracted, and it was soft stroking fingers that caressed my sensitive flesh. Satisfaction rolled through the familiar bond along with a love so deep it could fill the sea.

"I needed that," I breathed.

I could feel his lips twitch against my shoulder. "Best idea Damien ever had. I'll be sure to tell him."

CHAPTER 4
SAM

"Come on, little witch." Mathis pulled me toward the door. "I promised Eric, I would meet him there."

"No one's stopping you." It had been such a self-indulgent afternoon. Napping and making love, more napping, and a shower where I soaped his gorgeous body until he purred. For a little while all my problems had vanished. Right up until Mathis started his campaign to get me to go to the bar.

"You need to eat," he growled.

"Maybe I'll make a sandwich." The *maybe* kept it from being a lie. Most likely I wouldn't eat. Food was the last thing on my mind. "I have some things to check on the computer."

"Sam," Mathis crouched in front of me. "Is it the MS?"

I folded my arms over my chest and dodged with a snappish, "I'm more than my autoimmune disease, evil twin."

He glowered at me. I glared back at him. A battle of wills commenced a silent struggle. I broke first, throwing my hands up in the air.

"Fine. You're as bad as Damien. I'll make a smoothie right here in front of you, all right?" I headed into the kitchen and extracted berries and bananas from the freezer, and coconut water from the fridge. Mathis eyeballed me while I added flax seed to the single serving cup, and I glowered at him through narrowed eyes while the concoction blended together.

"You happy?" I transferred the mixture to a reusable cup with a straw and slurped all while casting him the hairy eyeball.

"You need protein." He folded his arms over his chest. So stubborn.

"I. Am. Fine." I snapped. "Don't look at me that way."

"What way?"

"Like you're disappointed in me."

"Never," he growled the word like a vow.

That mollified me a bit. He could be a pushy cajoling bastard, but he had his limits. "Or

more like my not wanting to go out is some sort of character flaw. I'm not twenty-five anymore, Mathis. There are nights I just don't want to deal with people."

He searched my face. "Okay, we'll stay in and starve."

"No, *we* won't. Go hang out with your brother. Get a burger. Or six." Shifter metabolisms burned up lots of fuel. "Damien will be home in an hour. I think I can keep out of trouble for that long."

I gave him a shove. He didn't budge of course.

Nothing in the universe got Mathis to move before he was damn good and ready.

"No work," he pointed a finger in my face. "Promise me."

"No work," I nodded. "I'll just watch some trash tv. I think there's a season of *90 Day Fiancé* I haven't seen yet."

He grimaced. "You have worse taste than Eric in entertainment. I didn't think that was possible."

I gripped the hem of his t-shirt. "Before you go insulting my superior taste, remember that I chose you, dumbass."

"Not something I'm likely to forget." He leaned in close, tucking the blanket around me, and brushed his lips over mine in an affectionate caress. "Love you, little witch."

"Love you too, you neurotic pain in my ass," I winked to take the sting out of my words and was rewarded with his husky chuckle and a hot kiss.

The second Mathis left, Wally and Wilma leapt onto the sectional to bookend me. Setting the smoothie on the coffee table, I grabbed the remote and tried to remember the channel number for Discovery. Or was that one of the add-ons for our streaming service? Goddamn, when had watching television become so freaking complicated?

A memory surfaced of trying to help my grandmother play a VHS rental. To my eleven-year-old brain, it had been a simple process. Put the television on channel three, push the tape in, and press play. Easy as pie. Not to Granny, though. The tech had intimidated her, a woman who had been a combat nurse during the second world war bested by a VCR.

And now I was the aging grandma made to feel stupid by smart technology and the fifteen remotes and input channels that my guys insisted on having even though it was rare that either of them watched television.

Turnabout's a bitch, Sam.

I swallowed and leaned back, closing my eyes. How long had it been since I'd even thought about my grandmother? Not since returning to the Outer Banks. She'd died when I was at college. Vividly I recalled the frantic call from my brother when he couldn't wake her up. Heart attack. It had been quick and painless. Not like my mom or Ray....

Nope, I shut that memory down hard. What was going on lately that my brain wanted to sashay down memory lane and kick rocks better left undisturbed?

Desperate for distraction I grabbed my phone. My finger hesitated on the email app. The urge to see if the Investor had responded strong. I'd promised Mathis I wouldn't work though. And keeping my promises was one of the few things I could do for my guys. Instead, I texted John, begging for baby Emily pics.

Three dots appeared.

John Moss: *They're on Instagram.*

I made a disgusted noise and wrote back,

Me: *Where any fucking pervert can find them.*

John Moss: *Mom, I have a private account.*
Me: *And how secure is that Mr. Hacker?*
John Moss: *Why are you giving me grief?*
Me: *I'm bored, and I promised Mathis I wouldn't work.*
John Moss: *So, watch TV.*
Me: *I don't know how. It's too complicated.*
John Moss: *Mom, I've got to go, Jessica needs help with the baby.*

"Liar," I typed back and said out loud, and then set the phone aside and looked at the corgis. "Do something entertaining. I'll make you YouTube stars."

They didn't even twitch. Lazy freeloading creatures.

I glanced at the clock. Damien would be another half an hour. I finished my smoothie with a straw suck and then set the cup aside. I wasn't hungry enough to deal with making a mess in the kitchen. Maybe I'd sit outside and wait for Damien and enjoy the ocean air and all that jazz.

After shooing Wally and Wilma down, I grabbed my cane and headed out the front door. And almost tripped over the bottle of wine someone had left on the porch.

"What?" I bent low and picked it up by the neck. My eyebrows rose when I saw the label. Pricy stuff. But good quality from a vineyard in the mountains.

"Damien?" I called out, wondering if it was something he had gotten for the restaurant. But why wouldn't he just bring it in? I carried the bottle inside and that's when I spied the sticky note.

Love, your secret admirer.

"Okay," I said the word slowly. Maybe it was my Swiss Cheese brain, but this secret admirer thing was starting to feel weird. Beyond weird. Not like Damien or Mathis. Those two would have signed their own names to any gifts. First the flowers now expensive wine. I had two shifter males in my life and everyone in the community knew it. So why would anyone be giving me gifts and signing them this way? Some sort of prank? The only one I thought might do that sort of thing was Eric, but he was so wrapped up in being newly married that I doubted he had time to mess with his brother. And he wouldn't want to upset Damien.

Odd as it felt, process of elimination said it had to be from one of the guys.

Didn't it?

"No shifter," the demon snapped over the conference call in Damien's office. "I have female troubles of my own. And as much as I enjoy verbally sparring with your witch, I know enough to never mix business with pleasure."

Damien scrubbed a hand over his face. "I appreciate your assistance. I know you're a busy man."

"Word of advice, Moss. Your mate is a powerful witch. And having the run of the convergence and all the supernatural beings within it will make her even more desirable. Guard what's yours ruthlessly."

"We plan to," Damien said and disconnected. It was odd, he never would have believed he would ever like a demon, but the Investor was an oddity. He seemed more and more human with every interaction. Almost as though he was...learning. Adapting to his new environment.

Damien wasn't ready to invite the creature to Thanksgiving dinner. That was just a foolish risk no witch or shifter with sense would take. Kind of like lying on a bed of vipers and expecting them not to bite.

He returned to his kitchen, waving to Sally O'Reilly the kitchen witch. Sally was a short, round woman with a twinkle in her blue eyes. The nights she helped him out in the restaurant the food had a little extra something special, though to his knowledge no one at *Second Chances* had been ensorcelled to date.

"Everything okay?" Sally asked as she minced onion with a practiced hand.

He nodded. "Sorry. My mind is elsewhere tonight."

"Young love." Sally sighed dramatically.

Damien chuckled. "Sally, you're barely a decade older than me."

"Yes, but Jim and I have been married for thirty years. Your relationship is still fresh. Plus, you have Mathis to deal with on top of everything."

Damien's lips curled. "Believe it or not, Mathis is a help."

"Oh, I believe it. I always said every woman should

have two men. One to cook and one to clean." She winked.

He shook his head and turned to the order slips. There were days Damien couldn't believe his life. Not very long ago he had given up hope of ever being with his mate or having a son. Or running his restaurant again after a hurricane and a fire had taken *the Sandpiper* down to the foundation. Now he had more than he ever imagined.

Gratitude was one of the lessons Alba had taught him. *People think happiness is a goal that they need to chase. But they're wrong. True contentment must be lured to you, like a skittish fawn. Do you want to be happy, son? Be thankful every day for what you have. Count your blessings and before you know it, happiness will come to you.*

Damien missed her. Yet he was grateful that she had picked him up, an abandoned cub along the side of the road. Who knew where he'd be now if not for Alba Moss's foresight and her great big heart?

The orders started pouring in and he and Sally moved with ease around the kitchen. This was what he'd been born to do, Damien thought as he tasted the gravy for his roast pork. Making food and loving Sam and Mathis. To shift with the full moon and to run along the beach with his pack, protected by the spells that kept humans ignorant of their true natures.

Perhaps he could convince Sam to participate in the next full moon revel. She was so tightly strung. Damien and Mathis did have to work as a team to keep her safe and happy. He smiled a little to himself as he cleaned the kitchen and shut off the lights. Maybe the universe did have some sort of cosmic plan in place. Sam needed them both, as familiars, as lovers. And as prickly as she could be, Mathis had a knack for cutting through her barbs and reaching the soft willing woman underneath. And for them there was nothing he wouldn't do in bed or out of it.

Sally headed out at nine, when he assured her he could close on his own.

After checking to make sure the dining room was set up for the next day, Damien shut off the lights and headed down to the parking lot. His truck was the only one in the lot. So why did he have the uneasy sense that someone was watching him?

Feigning ignorance, Damien took a deep breath, trying to scent if anyone or anything he recognized was nearby.

Nothing but the usual scents drifting on the sea breeze. Rot from the dumpster, the pungent tang of low tide, and the briny ocean air. No shifters or humans or gods forbid, demons. One was more than enough.

Still, his instincts were clamoring that someone was there. Watching him.

Instead of getting behind the wheel of his truck, Damien headed across the highway to the beach. As though his only aim was a stroll in the moonlight.

His ears pricked but he heard nothing unusual. All his well-honed senses reported the same thing. Nothing was there. And yet...

Damien reached into his pocket, trying to decide if he ought to call Mathis or Eric when something struck him in the back of the head.

His vision tunneled and the last thing he heard was a splash.

Mathis grabbed a beer from Javier before he joined Eric in the booth.

"Couldn't convince her to come?" His twin asked.

Mathis shook his head.

"Ginny's worried about her. She stopped showing up to morning yoga."

"She says she doesn't want to intrude on the newlyweds." Mathis rested his head back against the booth. "Can we talk about something else, please?"

Eric scowled at him. "Is something wrong?"

Mathis took a swig from his beer. "I'm more than just Sam's keeper, you know."

"Right," Eric said in a way that indicated it was anything but all right. "So...what *do* you want to talk about?"

"Fuck if I know." Mathis turned to stare up at the television in the age-old tradition of watching a sporting event.

He felt like a heel. He wanted Sam with him, participating in life, not hiding from it the way she was doing. MS stole her from him and Damien too often. And this creeping malaise that she'd sunk into had his guts clenching.

"I think she's grieving," Mathis said.

"Thought you didn't want to talk about it." Eric snarked.

Mathis ignored that. "I can't tell if it's John and Emily or Alba."

"Maybe it's her freedom," Eric suggested.

When Mathis scowled at him his twin held up both hands. "Don't bite my head off. I don't mean her single life or anything. But she's stuck here. She is forced to wait for people to come to her. That's a loss."

Mathis shook his head. "I don't—"

"Want to talk about it," Eric finished with him. "Yeah, I've heard that somewhere before."

Just then there was a commotion at the bar. Mel and Javier were having a heated back-and-forth.

"What's going on?" Mathis was on his feet.

Mel turned to face him. "Something just washed up on the beach."

"So?" Eric asked. "Stuff washes up all the time."

The true shifter's face was paler than usual as they said, "Yeah, but this smells like a body."

CHAPTER 5
SAM

The sound of an engine woke me out of a doze. "Finally, Damien." A glance at the clock confirmed it was well after midnight. He was more than an hour late. I clumped to the door and threw it wide. "I was starting to get—Oh, hi Ginny."

"Sam." Ginny Dunsany-Dracos as was an earth mother sort, all long flowing silvery hair and well-toned femininity. Usually, her expression was serene but in the porch light her expression appeared tense. "Eric just called me from the bar. Something washed up on the beach. The shifters think it's a body."

"A body," I repeated slowly. "As in a dead person?"

When Ginny nodded I swayed into the doorframe.

She caught me by the shoulders and glanced into the trailer. "Is Damien here? I didn't see his truck. According to Eric, Mathis can't get a hold of him." She referred to the telepathic link that connected the members of the pack.

"He hasn't come home." My gaze flew to hers. "What are you saying?"

Ginny held her hands up. "Absolutely nothing. The shifters want to know what you want them to do."

"Me?" I frowned.

She nodded. "You're the closest thing they have to an Alpha. As well as our coven leader."

I shut my eyes. Too much. The weight of it all, these people. I could barely handle myself, not make decisions about dead bodies. "Tell them to call the police."

Ginny hesitated. "If the death is supernatural in nature should we involve mortals?" Shifters and witches policed their own to help hide what they were from humans.

I reached for the phone and dialed Damien's number. My heart thudded against my ribcage. One ring. He was fine. Two. He had to be. Three. I would have felt something through the familiar bond if Damien was hurt. Four. Wouldn't I?

His voicemail picked up and I left a terse message. "Call me the second you get this."

Then I dialed Mathis. He answered on the first ring. "Sam."

"Where are you?"

"On the beach. With it."

Dread pooled in my guts. "Is it Damien?"

"I don't know." He hesitated. "There's no way to tell. It's all wrapped in a plastic trash bag and the scent is the ocean."

My eyes slid shut.

Ginny gripped me by the elbow. "Come sit down before you fall down."

My hands shook and it took effort to hold the phone up to my ear. "Mathis, we need to call the police."

"Sam," Mathis sounded cautious. I knew what he was thinking. What if one of us was at fault? We risked exposing the community to mortal scrutiny. We didn't want the police hovering around us.

My mind was sluggish, but I had enough presence of mind to ask, "Is there anything supernatural about the body?"

Mathis hesitated. "Nothing I can detect."

"Call the police," I repeated, more firmly. We'd get in more trouble if we called them in later, especially if rumors of witchcraft reached their ears. My witch wound, the psychic remembering of what people like me had endured at the hands of fearful humans, told me we did not want to cause a panic. We needed to come off as cooperative so that the authorities viewed us as a commune full of helpful kooks who danced naked under the full moon but still played by their rules. "Whatever you do, do not touch it or tamper with it or let anyone else mess around. Let the cops do their job."

Mathis knew an order when he heard one. "I will."

The sound of another vehicle had the corgis leaping up. Ginny and I turned to face the front of the trailer. Ginny pulled the curtain aside revealing the pickup pulling up in front of our porch. "It's Damien."

I expelled a heavy breath. "Damien's here."

"Thank all the gods," Mathis whispered. "I'll be home when I can."

A click sounded. I set the phone aside even as Damien staggered into the trailer. His white chef's coat was stained with rusty splotches and his salt and pepper hair was matted against his scalp.

"Damien!" I floundered to get to him. "What the hell happened?"

His pupils were blown, his blue gaze unfocused. He smelled of salt and sea and blood. He shook his head and winced as though the movement pained him. "I'm not sure."

My left side had picked a hell of a time to go numb. I lurched to one side. Ginny helped me up off the sofa, steadying me so I didn't faceplant into the living room rug. Despite his injuries, Damien caught me halfway. The second our skin made contact my healing magic sparked at my fingertips, assessing the damage.

"Why didn't you call us?" I chastised. "You shouldn't be driving like this."

"Had to get back to you," he rasped.

He had a concussion. My magic sank through his skin and down into his bloodstream, cataloging and making note of anything amiss. Someone had hit him on the back of the head. "Did you lose consciousness?"

He winced when I probed a tender spot with my fingers, checking to see if his skull had been fractured. "Can't remember."

I stepped away, leaning heavily on the kitchen counter for balance. "You need to lie down. Ginny, would you help him to the bedroom? I have a feeling the healing is going to knock him out cold."

Ginny nodded and put an arm around him. "Come on, big guy. Let's get you to bed."

I watched the two of them disappear down the hall. My hands were tacky from the clotting blood. Easing around the wall, I scrubbed up at the kitchen sink, checking to make sure they were clean before fumbling for the phone in my pocket. My left hand tingled so I put the device on the counter and with great effort texted Mathis. *Damien attacked. He has a head wound. Be careful!*

That done I fought the brain fog. What would I need for proper healing? I could just use my inborn white energy skill, but it would drain me dry. White light energy work took energy from the Healer as well as the person being healed. I didn't have any to spare. Amulets, talismans, and potions all aided in Healing, helping to amplify the energy we shared.

My witchy mini backpack sat on the counter where Mathis had left it when we'd come in earlier. I pawed through the contents like a bear at a picnic, choosing a white candle that I anointed with lavender oil. For a stone, I picked rose quartz, to symbolize the love I had for Damien.

Supplies ready, I lumbered toward the bedroom, using the wall to hold myself up. I'd crawl like my granddaughter if I had to but no matter what, I would heal Damien.

Ginny had laid a towel down over one of the pillows. Damien lay prone atop the covers, so I could reach the headwound.

Ginny gripped me by the shoulders and helped

support me to the bedside. Once I was seated she asked, "Do you want me to leave?"

I shook my head to clear it as much to answer her question. "I might need your assistance. Headwounds can be tricky." And if I poured too much magic into him there would be someone to look after Damien until his natural shifter resilience took over.

She nodded and stood back.

Hands shaking, I lit the candle and placed the stone beside it before letting my energy flow out of me and into Damien. The white light surged forward like waves lapping at the beach. That was how I always viewed a connection when I healed. My liquid light broke over and infiltrated the patient's immovable shore. I didn't know if other people could see the same things I did, had never had anyone to ask.

To me, Healing was like a dance. As the Healer I led, coaxing the shy patient's energy forth, enticing it to move and meld with my energy, like those little grains of sand that were drawn from the beach into the sea. My light would buoy the natural healing ability, speed it up, and strengthen it. Shifters healed faster than most and my familiars faster still.

The muscle spasms grew worse and it took all of my strength of will to remain upright. *You can rest later!* I told myself. *Damien needs you now!*

Minutes ground forward at a sluggish pace but gradually, the wound closed, the pressure was relieved, and the only sign that anything had been wrong was the dried blood in his hair and the towel beneath his head.

"What was that song?" Ginny asked me.

I'd forgotten she was there. "What song?"

"You were singing while you Healed him."

I blinked. "I was?"

She nodded. "It was beautiful. Ethereal. I couldn't understand the words but it lulled me like I was lying in a hammock that blew in the breeze. I felt totally relaxed."

I scrubbed a hand over my face. I'd been so focused on not collapsing in the middle of healing that I hadn't been aware of anything else. "I didn't realize I was doing anything. My focus was on getting him well." And not passing out.

I checked Damien's pulse. Strong and steady. Without the worry of internal swelling, we could both rest easy.

Ginny helped me up and together we went into the other room. I left the door cracked and the candle burning. I'd put it out when I went to bed.

"Where have you been, Sam?" Ginny asked softly.

I deliberately pretended to misunderstand. "You just got married, Gin. I'm trying to give you and Eric space. Besides, the B&B has kept me busy—"

Ginny held up a hand. "Sam, those excuses might work on your fellas, but believe me, honey, I have heard them all. You haven't been taking care of yourself."

"I'm fine."

"You missed an MRI."

I bristled. "How do you know that?"

She raised one elegant eyebrow. "I have my sources. Talk to me, Sam. Whatever you're hiding, it'll be easier if you let the community shoulder the burden with you."

I swallowed. "I'm afraid...it's gotten worse."

"It?"

"The MS. It's progressing. I've been so tired ever since I came here and I don't want to find out that it is worse because of..."

I held out my hands.

Ginny nodded. "Because of using magic."

I licked suddenly dry lips. "Because if it's true? If there's some unknown link between my Healing people and my worsening symptoms...I'm going to have to make a choice I don't want to have to make."

It was easy to talk to Ginny. She didn't judge, didn't drown you with sympathy, or urge you to change your thinking. She just listened and let you work shit out at your own pace.

"You know what your shifters will say," she murmured.

"Yeah." It didn't take a clairvoyant to figure out that Damien and Mathis would go ballistic every time I wanted to use magic if they believed there was a connection between my worsening symptoms and my mystical abilities.

I confessed a thought that had been waking me in the middle of the night. "I'm not afraid of dying, Ginny. But I'm terrified of being trapped and helpless in my own useless body."

Not able to heal Damien. Or to enjoy afternoons like the one I shared with Mathis. Existing but not really living anymore.

MS could change so much so fast. It was more than numbness or fatigue. It could take any path it wanted. Could rob me of the ability to write or walk or even talk clearly so I wouldn't even resemble the person I'd been. It could snatch my sex drive away like a thief in the night. At least Damien and Mathis would have each other if I dried up like an old husk.

That thought tanked my spirits further still.

"You can't keep the truth from them," Ginny spoke gently. "So, you'd rather pretend that it's all from overwork and let them make wrong assumptions. That's not healthy or fair, Sam."

I ducked my head, ashamed. She was only voicing what I already knew. I'd been living on borrowed time, playing pretend with all my might. But tonight proved that MS made me unreliable. As a leader, a Healer, and a mate.

The reckoning was nigh.

"I get the why." She put her hand over mine. "But just do everyone who loves you a favor? Stop avoiding us."

I swallowed even as my eyes misted. "I will. Or I won't. Oh hell, I'm too exhausted to focus."

She fetched my walking stick and handed it to me. "It's okay. Why don't you head to bed? I'll wait here for Mathis and Eric. The morning is soon enough to figure out what to do next."

"Sufficient unto the day is the evil therein?" I asked as I leaned heavily on the stick.

"Exactly." She winked. "Rest up, Healer. Tomorrow is another day."

Mathis watched as the police taped off the area where the body had washed ashore. Something itched beneath his skin. His cougar aspect wanted out, wanted to rend and tear and run home to protect his mate, not stand around like a useless lump while the mortal authorities did whatever they did by their short-sighted book.

"Any chance it was an accident?" Mel whispered from beside him.

"Wrapped in trash bags?" Eric hissed from his other side. "Unlikely."

"Quiet," Mathis snapped as the detective knelt over the bag and donned gloves.

"Is anyone missing from the community?" One of the deputies stopped in front of him, notebook in hand. "Any guests at the B&B gone missing?"

"No," Mathis shook his head. "The B&B is closed for renovations. And the community is all present and accounted for."

Thankfully because Damien had checked in with Sam. Mathis hoped he was sleeping off his recovery because come dawn, he was going to kick his ass for making them worry.

The body had been in the sea far too long for him to catch any sort of scent from it. The man doing the unveiling grimaced. Most likely, this wasn't a typical part of his job.

"Mel," Mathis hissed when the deputy wandered off. "See if you can get a closer look."

"On it." The true shifter stepped back into the shadows. Ivan and Fran Shevchenko came to stand beside him.

"You two found this?" Mathis asked to confirm what Mel had told him earlier.

Ivan rubbed a spot beneath his large, hooked nose and his Russian accent was strong as he muttered, "*Da.* Floating in the shallows. I used magic to drag it in closer while Fran went for the help."

Mathis watched the forensics photographer take pictures from every angle. No one noticed the crab that scuttled up along the plastic. Mel's gift truly did come in handy.

More unwrapping and then a rustle of plastic and the deputy handed something to the sheriff. A wallet. Would it contain identification of the victim?

He drank in every detail, knowing both Sam and Damien would want to hear it all several times over.

The deputy moved beside the sheriff and Mathis used his shifter hearing to eavesdrop on their conversation. The name they exchanged was one Mathis had never thought he would hear again.

Or had hoped he wouldn't.

He faded back when he spotted the crab scuttling his way. He didn't want to cause panic. His ears might have been playing tricks on him. In this world anything was possible. He clung to that thread like a lifeline.

Mel's gold sundress was draped over the railing that led from the deck of the bar to the main entrance, just out of view of the humans. Mathis leapt up and grabbed it and dropped it on top of the crab. They shifted and he waited impatiently for them to dress before asking, "Well?"

Mel's face was pale beneath the lights that crisscrossed in front of the bar. "It's him."

Shit. *Shit.* Robert fucking Sinclair. The energy vampire that had been Sam's husband. He'd seen the being only once over a year before as the Convergence took the energy vampire to feed itself. "How is that even possible? The convergence has never released anyone it's taken before. I saw it swallow him up."

Mel dusted sand from their white-blond hair. "I don't know. But there's more."

Mathis waited for the other shoe to drop. When it landed it was a stiletto right to his heart.

"There's a note written on his chest. In what smells like his blood. A note for Sam. Signed, Your Secret Admirer."

CHAPTER 6
SAM

I woke in the early dawn light to the feel of fingers in my hair and a murmured, "You all right, little witch?"

"Mathis?" And then I turned and saw the bed next to me was empty. I shot upright. "Damien?"

"In the shower. He wanted to get the blood off him." Mathis had a level of scruff going on that went hours past a five o'clock shadow and his eyes were bloodshot. "You slept for almost twelve hours. Did the Healing take it out of you?"

Instead of acknowledging the question I asked one of my own. "Did you get any sleep?"

When he shook his head I tried to tug him down beside me. To my surprise he resisted.

"What is it?" My eyebrows drew down as I stared up at him. "What's the matter?"

Instead of answering he backed away. "You should get dressed. The others are meeting us at Mel's in half an hour."

I'd never seen him so spooked. "Mathis, you're freaking me out. Just tell me what's going on."

He put his hands behind his head, biceps bunching beneath his tight black t-shirt. "Do you always have to be so stubborn?"

"Don't ask questions you already know the answers to," I snapped.

His arms dropped to swing by his sides and he glared at me. "Fine. This is a community-wide event because the body that washed up last night was spat out of the convergence. For the first time ever."

My lips parted.

"And," he continued. "Since it's connected to you, the police will probably be by sometime today to ask questions. We need to get our stories straight."

"Connected to me?" I stared at him.

"It's Robert, little witch." He swallowed, making the gesture look painful. "Robert Sinclair was fucking gift-wrapped by your secret admirer."

I stared at him for an endless moment. Trying to make sense out of the words. Robert. He'd been... devoured by mystical energy. How was there a body?

"This doesn't make any sense," I breathed.

The bathroom door opened and Damien strode out, naked and sopping wet.

Mathis swore. "You were listening?"

"Yes and I'll deal with you later," Damien snarled and then gripped my arms. "Firecracker, listen to me. He's dead. He can't hurt you anymore."

I nodded absently, not really hearing his words.

"Look at me." Damien ducked down until he could

catch my gaze. "Sam, he's dead. And whoever, or whatever, brought that body out is as good as dead. We won't let you be terrorized."

Something about the heat in his blue eyes woke me out of whatever trance I'd slipped into at hearing Robert's name.

"Secret admirer?" My teeth sank into my lower lip. "The one who sent the flowers? And the wine?"

"What wine?" Mathis snarled.

Shoot, with everything else that had happened the night before I hadn't told anyone. "It's on the counter. It was left on the porch."

"When did this happen?" Damien bared his teeth as he swung his head to face Mathis. Who was glaring at me as though it was my fault some sick fuck was terrorizing the community.

I cleared my throat. "Shortly after Mathis left."

"You left her alone?" Damien thundered.

"She wouldn't come out with me," Mathis snapped.

"Guys, don't fight," I pleaded.

They ignored me. Damien was crouched on the mattress and although he was still in human form he looked like a panther ready to spring. "You knew there was a potential threat and you abandoned our mate? I never should have trusted you with her."

Mathis looked as though Damien had sucker punched him.

I flailed until I could lay hands on Damien's bare arm. "Damien, stop. I told him to go out. It was practically an order."

"And what did he do that you felt the need to order

him away?" Damien turned that snarling countenance on me.

My brows drew together. "Nothing. You know better than that. I just didn't feel like going out and he was meeting Eric." I almost added it was perfectly safe, but it wasn't. Not after something had attacked Damien and delivered Robert's remains.

Mathis stood in the corner. His hands balled into fists and his big body shook with barely contained fury. "Is that really what you think of me?"

"I don't know what to think," Damien seethed. "I was attacked by what might as well have been a ghost for all I could detect it. And you knew there was something off with Sam. Did it really seem like the best course of action to leave her here alone with a target on her back?"

Evil twin's lip pulled back until he bared his teeth. "What was I supposed to do? Hogtie her and drag her to the bar?"

"If you had to," Damien said.

That broke Mathis's control. "Just because that's what you would do doesn't mean it's the right thing to do!" he thundered.

Tension crackled between them. "Guys, stop! We're getting nowhere."

Mathis turned to face me with an expression I hadn't seen on his face since the night we met. Rage and it was directed dead center at me. "This is your fault."

The blood drained from my face. "My fault?"

"Don't blame her for your lack of judgment," Damien

snapped. "She's probably as sick of your bullshit as I am!"

This time Mathis didn't look as though he'd been punched. He looked as if Damien had gutted him where he stood. Without a word, he stormed from the trailer.

I put my head in my hands. "Great Damien. That's fucking perfect. Go off on Mathis because you're afraid to be mad at me."

He was breathing hard.

"I know you sent Mel in as a spy. And I fucking resent that. At least Mathis is honest when he's pissed at me. He's not trying to wage some sort of secret campaign assuming I'm too stupid to figure out what's behind all the questions."

"Sam," he breathed.

I pointed to the door. "Don't give me that shit. I'll drive myself to Mel's. Just get out. And don't come back until you're ready to apologize to Mathis."

Damien stared at me for a long moment, his eyes full of fear and wariness. He wouldn't push. And I wouldn't demand an apology for myself. But I'd be damned if I let Mathis be his whipping boy.

"Out," I snarled.

He stalked to his closet, snagged clothes, and left.

I sagged onto the mattress and put my face in my hands. Mathis was right. This was my fault. And not because I had attracted yet another lunatic. I wasn't being honest with my guys, my community.

Or with myself.

That ended today.

I drove the Jeep down the beach and parked in front of Mel's. Jim O'Reilly was waiting to escort me up the steps to the bar.

"Looks like you drew the short straw, Jim," I told the shadow worker.

In his elderly leprechaun lilt he responded, "Nah, I volunteered. Your menfolk be in there glaring daggers at one another. No one wants to cross that kind of negative energy."

I heaved a sigh. "Perfect. Well, we might as well get this shitshow on the road."

Jim chucked me under the chin. "No worries, Sam. They get mad, they get glad."

I thought his take was a wee bit simplistic for beings that could sprout dagger-like teeth and claws to shred their enemies like a pulled pork sandwich but didn't say so. Jim and Sally were *hey, let's look on the bright side* sort of people, and I wasn't about to rain on his worldview that everything would work out all right in the end.

All eyes fixed on me when I clomped into the bar. Jim escorted me up to the stage where a high-backed chair had been placed. Nothing like being a spectacle. Even though I just heard about this meeting it was clear I was supposed to run it.

How had this even happened? I was no leader. This

was the group that Alba had gathered. I was a middle-aged Healer with a disease I had no way to cure.

To my left Mathis seethed. Through the familiar bond, I could sense his pain. He was like a scalded cat. To my right, Damien glowered, though not at me. He was still too wary that if I was upset, I'd show him the door. Tempers flared and everyone was on edge.

I needed to soothe them. There was only one way I was sure that I could.

Closing my eyes, I took a deep breath and began to sing. Maybe it was Jim's Irish accent that called the song to mind. U2's *With or Without You* poured out of me, echoed off the walls, and filled the space.

I could almost see the threads of music weaving through the crowd. Binding witches and shifters to one another. This was my community. I would fight for it. It didn't matter if I knew what I was doing. Someone had to hold the tether lines that connected us.

Damien's gaze had softened as he stared at me, his lips parted. He had always been particularly affected by my voice. I beckoned him forward. The song was my offering of apology. He'd been attacked last night, and a dominant shifter would take something like that personally.

He moved like a sleepwalker. One slow shambling step after the other. When he stood before me, I finished the song and gestured for him to stand by my side.

I cleared my throat and Mel hopped up and skirted around the bar where they poured me a glass of water.

"Thank you," I breathed when they handed it to me. I took a long sip and then rested the glass on my knee.

Mathis watched us from his corner, skulking in the shadows. Did he really think I would leave him out? We were beyond that.

Holding his gaze, I said loudly to the room. "I owe you all an apology. I don't know how to lead so I've been shirking the needs of this community. That ends now."

Mathis lifted his chin, the question in his eyes. I dipped my chin slightly so he would know that answers were forthcoming. Now wasn't the time or place. That was a discussion that needed to happen in private.

"Last night Damien was attacked outside *Second Chances*. Last night, a body washed up not ten yards from where we're standing. I haven't been part of this community long but I'm pretty sure that the two events are somehow linked."

Nods and murmurs of agreement.

I turned to Damien. "Can you tell us more about what happened?"

He drew a deep breath and then faced the room. "It was after closing. No one else was around. I had this feeling that I was being watched. But I couldn't scent anything."

More murmuring. It was well known in the community that Damien had the most sensitive nose of all the shifters.

Ginny rose from her chair. "I've had the same feeling."

"What?" Eric rounded on her, his dark eyes wide. "When?"

"The last few mornings," she confessed. "When I've been doing my yoga practice on the deck."

"Why didn't you tell me?" Eric appeared pained.

She leveled a look at her husband. "There was no proof. Just this unnerving sensation that I was being watched."

"I experienced it too," Fran piped up. "On my morning runs."

Ivan grunted, clearly not any happier than Eric that today was the first he was hearing about it..

"Anyone else?" I asked.

No one spoke up.

"Okay," I nodded. "Ivan, Fran, tell us about last night."

They did. The two of them had been out for an evening stroll when they'd come across the figure wrapped in garbage bags. Ivan had used magic to drag it out of the surf while Fran had run to Mel's for help.

"It's good that you didn't touch it," I told Ivan. "I told Mathis to telephone the mortal authorities and considering my connection to the dead man, I'm glad there's nothing else to link the death to anyone here."

"Is it really your ex-husband?" Bea asked, her Southern accent thick.

"I don't know. Most likely the police are going to ask me to identify the body."

Damien growled softly and I reached out to clasp his arm. "I promise, I won't go alone."

He cut his gaze to me, but at least the low growling sound stopped.

I faced the group again. "Shifters, we need you to reestablish patrols. You can work out a schedule amongst yourselves but there should be constant checks.

Bea, do you know how to set up a boundary spell like the one Alba had around us?"

When Bea nodded I continued. "Excellent. You're on that. Sally, please help her with anything she needs there. Ivan and Fran, I'm asking you both to research the convergence. I want to know if that really was Robert's body we're dealing with or an illusion spell of some kind."

Mathis frowned. Obviously, the idea that the body was an imposter hadn't occurred to him.

"Ginny and Jim, I'd like the two of you to help me with the B&B. I don't think it's a great idea to have crews in to work when we have a potential killer in the area but it's up to the Investor." I'd deal with the demon one way or another.

"And finally, no one goes anywhere alone. Not to work or on patrol or even walking home from the bar. If whatever is watching us is getting bold enough to attack one of our strongest members, I won't take the chance of them hurting anyone else."

"What about the police?" Javier asked. "What do we say to them?"

"If they ask, tell them the truth. You never met Robert Sinclair but you know I was married to him. And as far as you know he's never been to the B&B or the community."

The meeting broke up after that. The shifters congregated by the bar to work out a patrol schedule.

I focused on Ivan and Fran who approached me. Fran, a powerful hedge witch, had worked as a research librarian and was good at unearthing bits and bobs of information. Ivan was a conjurer. I wasn't all that certain of what his abilities entailed but he took his wife's direction well. It made them perfect for the job. "I need to know whatever you know or think you know about the convergence. I want a list of the people it has taken and if that happens anywhere else."

They nodded and then left. Ginny approached. In a low tone, she commented, "You did well, Sam. I don't know what you're so afraid of."

"Other than the ghost of my ex-husband?" I muttered.

She shook her head. "I didn't even consider that it might not be him."

"It doesn't matter," I said softly.

When she frowned I added, "Ginny, whoever this secret admirer is, they knew enough about me to know who my greatest enemy is. Whether they retrieved Robert from the convergence or killed a true shifter to make the being look like him, or it's some sort of elaborate ruse, they've been watching me for a long time. Since before I came here. Unearthing Robert is a threat. They might even know I was instrumental in his death."

Her eyes widened. "So, what do we do?"

I shook my head. "We collect information. We protect ourselves and each other. And we prepare."

I only hoped it would be enough.

CHAPTER
SEVEN

Damien waited until the patrol schedule had been sorted before he pulled Mathis aside. "We need to talk."

Mathis folded his arms over his chest and glared. Damien recognized the stubborn lift to his chin, hated to see the wariness return to Mathis's dark eyes. He'd fucked up royally by accusing Mathis of taking Sam's safety for granted. Damien scrubbed a hand over his face as he hunted for the right words. Being inside the bar where everyone could overhear made him edgy. "Can we go outside?"

A single nod was his only response. Mathis followed him out onto the deck. The wind had picked up and Damien stood for a long moment, breathing in the briny air before turning to the other shifter. "I was wrong to blame you. I'm scared for her and I lashed out."

One sardonic eyebrow lifted. "Scared for her or scared of her?"

Damien shut his eyes. "Maybe both. She's left me

before. And even though the past few months have been amazing the knowledge that I could still fuck this up, that I could lose her, haunts me."

Mathis let his arms fall to his sides, his ridged stance easing slightly.

So Damien kept going. "You don't know what it's like to be without her. And it's not just her I'm afraid of driving away."

The other shifter's lips parted but he made no sound.

Delving for his courage Damien confessed, "It's not just a game or kinky sex. It hasn't been for a long time."

"What are you saying?" Mathis whispered.

Something he should have said a long time ago. "I love you, fool. And not because of Sam or any of the fucked-up stuff that brought us to where we are. You're at the center of my heart, right next to her. I might survive losing one of you, but not both."

One moment they were standing six feet apart and in the next, Mathis had his arms around Damien. Breath shuddered out of him as he clung to the man who had invaded his heart and soul with the same sneaky guile as the woman who was the mother of his son.

"Get a room!" Eric called from behind them.

Mathis released him and they both turned to snarl at the other cougar. Eric rolled his eyes, but he smiled at them. "Took you morons long enough. Fucking alphaholes."

A chuckle escaped Damien.

"So, when's the ceremony?" Eric asked.

"Ceremony?" Mathis scowled.

"Uh, yeah, if you wanna keep it, you gotta put a ring

on it." He held up his left hand, letting his gold wedding band catch the hazy sunlight.

Damien blinked and looked at Mathis.

Mathis seemed to be thinking it through. "Would it make you feel better if we bound her to us that way?"

Fear gripped Damien. "What if she says no?"

Mathis gave him a hard gaze. "Then we'll have to convince her to change her mind."

Damien shook his head. "You make it sound so easy."

"Nothing about that woman is easy," Mathis replied. "Just like nothing about you has ever been easy. But I think you're both worth fighting for."

Tension he hadn't even realized he'd been carrying left Damien in a rush. He nodded. "All right. Just not today."

"Not today, Mathis agreed. "Today we need answers so we can keep her safe."

Sam

GINNY AND JIM rode with me along the shoreline on our way to the B&B. I'd been planning to talk with Damien and Mathis but the two of them had agreed to be on first patrol. And I needed to be on tap for the police and their questions.

"You told us we should tell the truth or at least part

of the truth," Ginny pointed out. "But what are you going to say?"

"The same. That I left Robert more than a year ago." My stomach twisted at the thought of detailing the abuse he'd heaped on me or how John had to basically abduct me to get me to leave the garbage situation. But I had to convince the authorities to look elsewhere.

The sheriff's car was waiting for us at the B&B. Two deputies exited the vehicle as I parked in the gravel lot. One was older, doughier with a thick salt and pepper mustache. He looked friendly. Ah, the good cop. Which meant...my gaze tracked over to the other one. In his mid-thirties, though I guessed he could be younger. Thin with no muscle, he had a baby face and mean eyes. Yep, he was definitely going to be bad cop.

I made a show of using my walking stick as I got out of the Jeep and headed toward them. Hey, if the sympathy vote kept them from hauling me in for questioning, then I would exploit my own weakness.

"Gentlemen," I offered a friendly smile. "What can I do for you?"

"Are you Samantha Sinclair?" The older deputy asked.

I nodded. "I am."

"And your husband is Robert Sinclair?" His eyes were a very pale gray as he gauged my reaction.

"Ex-husband," I corrected abruptly. "We've been divorced for a while now."

"Yeah, I hear she's shacked up with two guys," the other deputy eyed me up and down. It was clear from his expression he wondered what exactly it was about me that could attract a lover, let alone two.

Ginny put herself in front of me. "I don't see what Sam's living situation has to do with anything. Or are you just looking for confirmation for your spank bank?"

Jim made a choking sort of sound even as the baby-faced deputy turned bright red.

The older deputy cleared his throat and made a valiant attempt to redirect the conversation. "When was the last time you saw your ex-husband, Ms. Sinclair?"

"The day I left him," I lied smoothly. "Our divorce was handled through my lawyer's office."

A nod of acknowledgment and he scribbled something on the pad.

"What's this all about?" I asked in my best clueless simp voice.

The older one offered me a slightly sympathetic look. "A body carrying your ex-husband's ID card washed up on shore not too far from here."

"What?" I covered my mouth as though I was shocked and shook my head even as I registered that the man hadn't confirmed that it was Robert.

Baby-face piped up, "Are you aware that your lover, Mathis Dracos has a criminal record?"

My head snapped up and this time the surprise wasn't feigned. "What?"

Mathis, I thought. *What the fuck did you do?*

"He served six months in Mississippi state facility for aggravated assault."

Ginny had her arm around me and said, "I don't see what that's got to do with anything."

Baby-face glared at her. "We're asking the questions here."

I gripped her arm and Jim moved forward. "Gentlemen, Ms. Sinclair has had a terrible shock. She'll come later and give a statement but unless she's under arrest, I'd recommend that you head out."

"She's not under arrest." The older one cast a glare at his younger counterpart as though the younger man had gone and done something he'd been specifically warned not to do. "We appreciate your assistance. Come to the Sheriff's office and give your statement before the end of the day."

My head spun and if not for Ginny's support I would have sunk down onto the handicap ramp.

"Help me get her inside," Ginny said to Jim.

Together they guided me up the ramp. Jim took the keys from me and unlocked the front door. The smell of sawdust greeted us. A comforting aroma.

"Do you want me to call Mathis or Damien?" Jim asked.

"No, that's all right." I forced a smile.

"Maybe a cup of tea?" Ginny suggested.

I nodded even as I searched her eyes. She didn't look surprised about Mathis. Eric had probably told her.

I needed to talk to Mathis. Before I spoke with the police. Damn it, why hadn't he told me?

Reticent evil twin and all his damn secrets. I shook my head and picked up the phone.

I had a demon to talk to.

"No," The investor told me over the video conference. "I grow weary of these delays, Samantha Jean Sinclair. You assured me the grand opening would happen on time and on schedule. I have arranged for important influential people to come to see the place. I don't care whom I must bribe or how many bodies wash up on the shore. *The Sawgrass* is opening a week from Saturday. Period."

"Be reasonable," I pleaded with the demon, knowing it was useless.

"I have been very reasonable. I even put up with one of your pets calling to accuse me of sending you flowers yesterday. But now I'm feeling irritated."

I stilled. "Damien called you?"

"Yes, and I don't appreciate the accusation from a jealous shifter. One whom I've helped and whose woman I employ. I've learned enough about your world to understand that sexual harassment lawsuits are a special level of hell."

"I'm so sorry," I breathed. "It won't happen again."

The demon made a disgruntled sound. "A week from Saturday, Ms. Sinclair. Or I'll find myself a new manager." There was a click and he was gone.

I hung up the phone and set it aside. Ginny and Jim were staring at me with sympathy.

"There's no way this is going to happen." I breathed.

"Unless," Jim tapped the side of his bulbous nose. "We throw a few spells around?"

My teeth sank into my lower lip. "Is it safe?"

Ginny drummed her fingers on the tabletop. "We can be careful to use magic outside of the convergence. I'm more concerned about the personal gain aspect."

There were three types of magical practitioners. White witches practiced for the benefit of others. As a Healer that was primarily what I did. Shadow workers like Jim also. He'd helped me come to terms with trauma from my past. Personal gain was a big no-no in the witch community. It was one thing to heal or to draw power from the full moon. Another entirely to do things to only benefit yourself. If you cast a spell for personal gain, your status as a white witch would be revoked. You could no longer do white witch spells.

"I can't risk it," I told them. As an energy worker, there was no telling what would happen if I lost my white witch status.

"We could do it for you. Or rather, I could." Ginny was a green witch. While most of her magic use was benign, she did dabble in gray areas from time to time.

I shook my head. "I couldn't ask you to do that."

"You aren't asking, Sam. I'm offering. I'll get Fran to help me."

I frowned. Fran was a hedge witch. "Fran practices gray magic?"

Jim and Ginny exchanged a glance and Jim said "No, Sam. Fran practices the dark arts."

I blinked. "Black magic? Since when?"

"Since always," Ginny sighed. "It's not something she

talks about very often, but it's sort of an open secret. We all know about it."

Everyone except me, apparently. Black magic meant that the practitioner no longer operated under the *and harm to none do as though wilt* motto. Black magic included compulsion spells to bend others to your will, stealing another's magic, and summoning demons.

Fran had a bit of a sinister air about her but I never would have imagined she would do any of those things. She was a bookworm who spent most of her days at the library.

"If it makes you uncomfortable," Jim began.

I held up my hand. "I'm working for a demon. I think dabbling in the darkness is inevitable. Gin, if you and Fran are willing, I'd appreciate all the help I can get."

Ginny called Eric and a few minutes later Mathis's twin appeared in mountain lion form to escort his lady to find Fran.

"You knew Alba practiced the dark arts too?" Jim said.

And the hits just kept on coming. "What?"

He gave me a kind smile. "No one saw that either. It was why Fran felt comfortable here. Alba used compulsion spells all the time. It was what protected us whenever a mortal saw a mountain lion hundreds of miles from where a mountain lion should be."

I shook my head. "That doesn't sound like black magic."

Jim shrugged. "Anything that messes with a living being's free will is part of the dark arts, Sam. Remember that."

As we settled in to go over the massive task list that needed to be handled before the grand opening, I told myself I was unlikely to ever forget.

Damien and Mathis ran along the beach in their cougar aspects. Other than where the body had been, and the smell of mortal law enforcement, all the scents were from members of the community. Damien shifted back as they hit the edge of the convergence. "There's nothing here."

Mathis stared up at him and Damien's lips twitched. "All right. I want to see her too. Let's head to the B&B."

He was worried about Sam. Could feel Mathis's worry too. Whatever secret she was keeping from them was weighing on her mind. Anything that came between the three of them must be dealt with swiftly. Damien still regretted his explosion from earlier that day. He'd make it up to Mathis and to Sam. Somehow.

When they arrived at the B&B, they spied Sam's Jeep. Sam herself was nowhere to be seen, but Jim was seated at the front desk.

"Where is she?" Damien asked as he reached for the duffel bag full of sweats that they kept on hand for shifters.

"She went to the ladies' room." Jim eyed the two of them for a long moment. "The mortal police were giving her a hard time and the demon won't push back the grand opening. She's not having the best of days."

When Mathis cursed the older man's eyes focused on him. "She's also upset about something the police told her regarding you doing time for aggravated assault."

Mathis stilled.

"What?" Damien spun to face Mathis. "When?"

Shifters didn't do well behind bars. The beast would go mad at the thought of being controlled or caged.

Mathis didn't answer. Instead, he barreled toward the hall bathroom wearing only a pair of sweats. He pounded on the bathroom door. "Sam!"

Damien followed him and gripped him by the shoulder. "Give her a minute."

Mathis shrugged him off and continued abusing the newly installed door, this time by jiggling the handle. "Samantha Sinclair, open this door."

Damien tried to reach out through the familiar bond to get a hint of Sam's mood. Was she angry? Upset?

He couldn't feel anything at all. That wasn't right. He should feel something.

Mathis had quit playing nice. "Sam if you can hear me stand back." He shoved his shoulder into the wood. A loud crack filled the space as the lock gave way. The door rebounded off the wall and Damien caught it before it could slam into Mathis.

Sam lay on the tiled floor, unconscious.

CHAPTER 8
SAM

"Mom?" I called as I walked through my grandmother's house. Everything was the same. Nothing had changed since the day the three of us moved in with our mother's mother. "Where are you?"

The couch was an ugly orange and teal fabric, Scotch guarded to within an inch of its life. A fire blazed in the fireplace and the smell of woodsmoke would cling to my clothes and hair long after I left the house.

"Mom?" Continuing past the living room I moved down the hall to the bedrooms. The door stood ajar. I pushed it inward and spied her there, her eyes closed, her face drawn. She was thin, her skin waxy and sheened with sweat. Her eyes were sunken into her skull and her lips dry and cracked. The calling card of illness.

I moved to sit beside the bed and took her hand in mine. Her skin felt papery and was so thin I could follow the line of every vein. "Mom? It's me. It's Sam."

Her lash-less lids lifted. She stared at me for a long moment. "Sam?"

I swallowed hard. "Yeah, Mom. I'm here."

I hated being there. Incapable of doing anything to make her better. Yet where else should I be?

Mom regained focus and her blue eyes seemed to burn as she peered into my depths. "My Samantha Jean. You're special. You and Ray. You need to look out for him."

She wasn't making any sense at all but she seemed so upset that I said, "I will. Of course I will. Don't worry. You don't have anything to worry about."

It wasn't a lie. My brother Ray was at school because I made him go even though he wanted to be here at this ongoing deathwatch.

She coughed, the spasms rocking her frail frame. She'd lost so much weight.

I reached for the water that the day nurse had left within easy reach and aimed the straw for her cracked lips. She batted it away. "No. It's poisoned."

"Mom, it is not," I said, exasperated, and brought the cup to my own lips.

"No!" With surprising strength, she knocked it out of my hands. Water soaked the bedding even as the plastic cup skittered across the pink shag carpet.

I rose intending to pull the wet fabric away from her but she gripped my hands with a strength I didn't think she still possessed. "Water will be your salvation. Water will be your doom. You need to know the truth about your father, Sam. You must know what you are."

"What I am?" My heart pounded. No one ever talked

about our father. Not our mother and not Gran. I had no memory of him and the few times I'd asked, I'd been redirected. My questions dismissed. "What are you talking about?"

"Sam?" Someone was calling my name. Ray must be home from school.

"Mom, talk to me. Tell me what you meant. What about our father? What do we need to know?"

"Sam!" Hands on my shoulders shook me.

I shrugged them off. "Not now, Ray. This is important."

Another sharp shake. I tried to focus on Mom, but she was fading into the bed, which merged with the wall. The house melted away. My lids lifted.

And I stared up into Mathis's wild dark eyes.

"What?" I breathed as my surroundings came into focus. I wasn't in my grandmother's house. I was sprawled out on the bathroom floor of the B&B.

Mathis hauled me against him, squeezing me with superhuman strength.

"Easy." Damien's voice was firm and full of command. "Give her room to breathe."

Mathis relaxed his suffocating grip only a little. "Damn it, little witch. You scared the hell out of me."

Part of me still sat beside my mother's bed hungering for answers. My brows drew together as I looked up at Damien. "What happened?"

It was Jim, hovering in the doorway who answered. "You went to the loo and didn't come back out. I was just starting to wonder if you fell in when these two showed up and went all Hulk-smash on the new powder room."

My eyes flitted back and forth as I tried to remember. I'd come into the bathroom, did my business, and then propped my walking stick by the door so I could wash my hands. I had a vivid memory of staring down at the water as it ran through my fingers. Vertigo swamped me, my balance gone. And then...

Blank spot. As though whatever happened next had been erased.

My gaze landed on the broken door frame and I shoved at Mathis. "Was that really necessary?"

"You didn't answer." He was breathing too fast. As though he'd been flat-out sprinting. Waves of anxiety buffeted me through the familiar bond. "Jim said the cops were here and neither of us could feel you."

He meant through the bond. When I slept they couldn't sense my emotions. But what the hell had put me into that trance?

I needed to focus. What was Mathis upset about? The investigation. Robert. "Earlier yeah. I'm supposed to go give a statement." I studied the strain around his dark eyes. "Come with me?

"We should get you to the doctor." Damien's blue eyes assessed me.

But I shook my head. "No, I'm fine. Help me up."

"Sam," Mathis began.

"I said I'm fine." Or at least as fine as possible. "Let's go to the police station and get that over with. We want to demonstrate cooperation. Jim, you have all the info to pass on to Fran and Ginny?"

When the shadow worker nodded, I said. "Good. We'll drop you at the library and then head into town."

"Sam," Mathis rasped and I shot him a warning look. Not now while I was sitting on the bathroom floor in front of Jim. We had too many problems and no time to deal with them all before the demon's deadline.

Jim shut down the computer and I locked the B&B and then the three of us piled into the Jeep. Damien, dominant that he was, insisted on driving. I let him, my gaze on the crashing waves.

It had happened before—vertigo. No tingling, no numbness, no warning at all. The world tilted and then... nothingness. The blank spot in my mind meant MS had punched a new hole in my Swiss cheese brain. But was the fainting spell a new symptom? Or something else?

And the memory... I never recalled what I dreamed about. But I hadn't been dreaming. I'd relived an event from my past. Mom's cryptic warning and the one and only mention of my father.

Damien parked in front of the library. "I'll go in with Jim. You two wait here."

I nodded absently. They were just out of earshot when Mathis leaned over the front seat. "The cops told you about my record?"

"It doesn't matter," I whispered.

His chest rose and fell, his breathing choppy. "I should have told you about it a long time ago."

I turned to face him. "Does Damien know?"

He hesitated. "He does now."

It didn't make sense. "Why wouldn't you tell him?"

"It's not something I'm proud of. Alba knew. It was how we met."

"Sounds like there's a story there," Sam murmured.

Mathis stared into Sam's clear blue eyes. They looked even brighter offset by the dark circles beneath them. Even with twelve hours of sleep, she didn't appear rested. His throat closed. Yeah, there was a story. And maybe sharing it would convince his little witch that she could reveal her concerns to him.

She covered his hand with hers. "You don't need to tell me about this if it's uncomfortable for you to talk about."

Uncomfortable? He wanted to weep. The sense of panic that he'd felt when Jim had said the mortal authorities spilled the beans to Sam about his record hadn't eased. He thought for sure she'd run, as any sane woman would when she learned her lover had a record for aggravated assault. Finding her unconscious on the bathroom floor hadn't done a thing to settle his nerves.

He brought her soft, cold hand to his face. Her fingers were so slender and pale. There were times he thought she was on the verge of fading into the shadows, as though she wasn't flesh and blood, but some sort of ethereal creature come to life to ease him.

He swallowed thickly. "It was after Eric and I left our former pack."

"You mean, after they turned on Eric?" She whispered.

He nodded. She knew a great deal of the story, how he'd been used as a placebo to sexually satisfy the alpha whose mate had rejected him. How that same female had flirted with Eric and the pack had held Mathis back, preventing him from helping his brother as the male that had used Mathis savaged him and left him short one eye and on the verge of death.

"We had no money, no place to stay. Eric was badly hurt. You know the difference between being poor and being impoverished?"

When she shook her head, he explained. "Poor means you lack resources. Impoverished means you lack hope. There was no one to help us. And when our former alpha found out Eric had managed to survive, he put a price on his head."

Her lips parted but she said nothing, just listened and let him blunder through at his own pace.

"We were camped out under a bridge in cougar form because it was both warmer and easier to find food that way. We hadn't eaten a cooked meal in months. Eric couldn't hunt because of the blind side so it was up to me to find enough to keep us both alive." He swallowed past the lump in his throat. "I didn't think he was going to make it."

Sam turned her face and pressed a kiss into his palm. It was a small, sweet gesture that gave him the courage to continue.

"Anyway, I was out hunting when I sensed them nearby. I hurried back to the bridge and found Eric in human form. If we get too weak we can't hold the animal aspect. And there was a man there. He had a knife to my brother's throat."

Mathis closed his eyes as the memory assaulted him. The rage that had washed over him at the sight.

"I didn't recognize him. Didn't stop to think or even use my nose. I launched myself at him. He slashed out with the knife and cut me here." He traced the long scar that bisected his left pectoral.

"My god," Sam shook her head. "Mathis—"

"I lost enough blood that I had to change back. So the cops found me in human form, beating him into unconsciousness."

Sam's eyes turned wet. "You were protecting your brother."

He shook his head. "That's not it,"

"Then what?"

"The man. He was homeless. Schizophrenic. Not even a shifter. He wasn't really a threat but I beat him to within an inch of his life. The same way my brother had been beaten. It could so easily have been a murder conviction."

There were tears in her blue eyes. "Damien told me that shifters don't do well behind bars."

Mathis let out a humorless laugh. "No, we don't. And I would probably have died in there if not for Alba. She collected Eric and brought him back here. Hired a lawyer for me. He couldn't get me out entirely but managed to convince the judge to reduce the sentence. It was rough, but I survived."

A tear tracked down her cheek. "I'm so sorry."

"Not as sorry as I am."

She sniffled and then gripped his hand and held it to her face. "Thank you for telling me. And I can feel your apprehension. What is it you're worried about?"

He studied her gaze. "That you'll think I'm some sort of loose cannon. Or a scumbag who beats on helpless people."

"You were protecting your brother. God, Mathis. Who knows what that man would have done to Eric? For all you know, he saw him shift and was frightened enough to kill him."

Mathis had considered it many times. What would have happened if he had come back five minutes sooner? Or five minutes later? Alba had helped him through that.

"Damien's afraid he's going to drive you away. But he's not a goddamned convict."

Another squeeze of her hand. "I love you. Nothing will change that. Nothing."

His breathing was ragged as he leaned forward and slid his fingers into her hair. "Same, little witch."

Her gaze darted then, as though checking for a trap. "I'm not...I don't—"

He kissed her. Trying to reassure her and ease her distress. His tongue swept into her mouth in a possessive claim.

The car door opened and Mathis released her, rubbing his thumb along her silky locks.

"Am I missing something?" Damien asked.

Sam was panting for breath but she shook her head. "You two can talk about it while I give my statement."

Mathis leaned back against the headrest and shut his

eyes. The only thing worse than re-living his past for a loved one? Having to do it twice.

"You're not off the hook, little witch," he warned.

Sam turned back to the window. "I know. I promise we'll all talk about it tonight."

CHAPTER 9
SAM

My official statement stuck to what I'd told the two deputies when I'd been questioned. No, I hadn't seen Robert Sinclair since I left him. I hadn't heard from him either. Yes, he was abusive. No Mathis wouldn't have gone after him.

"Do you want me to identify the body?" It took no effort to make my voice shake. I really didn't want to see what was left of Robert after the convergence was done with him.

"That won't be necessary, Ma'am." The older deputy thanked me and I was free to go.

Damien and Mathis had been waiting in the lobby for me. They sprang up when they saw me but I subtly shook my head. I wondered if Mathis would be questioned as well.

"Shouldn't you be at work?" I asked Damien once we were heading back to the beach.

Damien shrugged. "It's a weekday anyway and business has been slow. I don't want to risk any of my employees getting attacked."

I nodded, glad I wouldn't have to worry about him that night.

Though I was exhausted and leaning heavily on my cane and my shifters, I owed them an explanation.

When we were situated out on the deck they both looked at me expectantly. Wally and Wilma happily dug in the warm sand. I fidgeted with a linen placemat. "I should be doing something."

"Firecracker," Damien said in a tone that was filled with both exasperation and patience.

"I know, it's just a feeling." There was nothing I could do, other than wait for

Ginny and Fran to compel some contractors and inspectors to hurry up on the B&B.

"It's easier once you get going," Mathis vowed.

I looked at him and he nodded slightly. He had talked to Damien about his criminal record. Taking a long breath, I plunged into the deep end. "Okay, so here's the thing. I skipped my last MRI."

Both shifters stiffened. Before either could ask why I added, "And no, it wasn't an accident."

"I'm not sure I understand," Damien said slowly.

"At my last appointment the doctors said that there was nothing they could do. The meds haven't been working. I've been having...lapses." I tried to explain. "There are gaps in my head. It's part of what's been making me so crazy about the renovations. I forget if I've done something so I'm double and triple checking. You've probably noticed." I directed the last part to Mathis.

His dark brows drew together. "I have. I thought you were being overly cautious."

"There's more." Unable to look at either of them I turned my gaze out to the ocean. "When I sleep I'm... remembering things. Scenes from my past. How my mother died. At first, I thought losing Alba had brought it all up. That it was just grief that needed to be endured. But today...that memory took me under. I couldn't fight it, didn't even know what was happening until it was too late."

Mathis swore. "Sam, if you'd been driving.... You could have been killed."

"I know," I whispered. "And I won't drive or do anything else that puts me or anyone else in harm's way." Not until we figured out what was happening.

Damien rose and began to pace. "Why didn't you tell us?"

I licked suddenly dry lips. *Rip it off, Sam. Like a Band-Aid.*

"Because it's getting worse since I've been here. And I think that maybe when I Heal people...it's been taking more from me than I realized."

Mathis lunged forward and gripped my hand. "What?"

"The fatigue, that's normal. At least normal for me. But the dizzy spells and the zoning out, the vertigo and the memory lapses." I shook my head.

Damien crouched by my side. "You need to go to the doctor. They might be able to help you."

"They'll tinker with my meds. Order more tests. But between what happened to you last night and then the episode today I'm convinced it's not MS related." I explained about the memory of my mother.

"The water will be your salvation?" Damien repeated. "What was she talking about?"

"I don't know."

Mathis asked, "What was her official diagnosis?"

"She never had one. Neither did Ray. No insurance." Although I was beginning to suspect MS or something that mimicked it symptom-wise was in the mix.

Damien bowed his head. I saw Mathis get up and wrap an arm around him for comfort. Damien leaned into the touch. The sight of them supporting each other gave me comfort. They needed to do that more. Especially—

"Don't you dare," Mathis growled and turned to face me. "You are not allowed to check out."

I blinked as I looked up at him. "I'm not."

"You have been," he snarled. "You absolutely have been. It's why you've been avoiding the community, isn't it? Getting us all used to your absence? Like we will miss you less if you put up these gods damned walls!" He gripped a large shell that we'd been using to hold down napkins and flung it with all his strength into the sea. Wally and Wilma barked and raced after it.

Damien was staring at me with dawning horror. "You don't...think you're... dying?"

"I don't know." It was the truth.

"No," Mathis growled. "No, Sam. Damn it, do not give up."

I shook my head. "You don't know how it went. For

my mother, for Ray. They were so strong...until they weren't."

Damien's chest was heaving, his blue eyes bright. "There must be more to this. Your mother talked about the water being your salvation."

"And also my doom," I reminded him.

Mathis pointed a finger in my face. "We'll figure it out. You don't get to give up. You have more fight in you. I won't fucking let you."

Damien moved to stand shoulder-to-shoulder with him. "And until we do, no more Healing."

Damn it, I knew they'd pull this shit. "Look, there's no proof I am dying. MS isn't usually fatal."

"But you don't know what this is," Damien pointed out. "Because you won't go to the damn doctor."

I shut my eyes. "You can't keep me from doing what I was put here to do on a whim. What if it costs someone their life? What if it's one of you? Or Ginny or Eric? What if it's Emily whose life hangs in the balance? Do you honestly think I could go on knowing I had the power to help and I let someone I love die?"

Ray and my mother were bad enough. I hadn't been able to tap my gifts then. Had no idea I was a witch or a Healer or anything special. But my mom knew. Had she been trying to tell me where to go? What to do?

I rose slowly and leveled my gaze on both the men I loved. "I'm not giving up. I know how to adjust and make compromises. And I will for as long as I can. I'm not ready to let either of you go. Now, it's been a long day and I'm tired. So good night."

They didn't try to stop me as I whistled for Wally and

Wilma. Neither of them said a word as I made my way into the trailer. I showered and then still in my bathrobe, fell into bed.

And sobbed.

DAMIEN PACED the length of the deck. He wanted to run. But he couldn't. It wasn't safe, not with whatever had gotten the drop on him skulking around out there. Mathis sat in the shadows of the steps, watching the crescent moon rise. His energy was a black hole sucking up all the air around them.

"Stubborn little witch," he murmured at one point.

Damien had to agree. Sam was a grown-ass woman. If she didn't want to go see a doctor he couldn't force her to go. A brief fantasy of hogtying her and dragging her to the hospital emerged and he snorted.

"What could possibly be funny?" Mathis snarled.

"I just imagined dragging Sam kicking and screaming to the doctor."

Mathis raised a brow. "I might help you."

Damien shook his head. "We don't know what's going on yet. And we won't until we convince her to go there."

"What if she's right though? Mathis asked. "What if Healing others is making her worse?"

"Then she'll have to adapt. She said she would. If I'd known, I would have insisted she leave me to the concussion last night."

Mathis glared at him.

"What?"

Mathis rose. His turn to pace. "Damien, you heard her. If someone she cares about is hurting Sam will do whatever is in her power to fix it whatever it costs her."

Damien knew that. But he couldn't accept it. He could beg. Part of him wanted to do it right this second. Beg her to turn to mortal medicine. And if they couldn't find the cause of her symptoms, then beg her never to Heal anyone ever again.

But what if it was John? Or Emily? His inner voice whispered. Could he really watch them suffer?

"There's only one thing we can do," Mathis turned to look at him.

"What's that?"

Mathis lifted his chin, his jaw set at a stubborn angle. Handsome devil. Sam had been right to nickname him evil twin. There was something sinister glinting in Mathis's eyes. "We have to find Sam's father."

"Where do we even start?" Damien asked.

Mathis didn't answer directly. Instead, he pulled out his phone and shot out a text. A moment later the phone pinged.

"Who are you texting?"

"The only person I know who can find someone who doesn't want to be found," Mathis snarled. "Your son."

Sam

Neither of them came to bed. I missed being held by my shifters but understood I brought this on myself. It was my fault after all. I shouldn't have been keeping secrets, not even to spare them worry or pain.

I stared out the large plate glass window at the gray morning. This time the dream/memory featured Ray lying in the bed, babbling nonsense at me. *Did you ever wonder where we came from? Why we are the way we are?*

At the time I thought it was just fever dreams, grasping at straws. Kinda like what I was doing now. Couldn't drive. Couldn't walk smoothly. Lack of appetite. Had I even eaten the day before? It proved how distracted Damien had been that he hadn't been shoving food at me.

Magic or medicine? Which was doing me dirty?

It wasn't just the fear of having my hands bound when it came to Healing. I couldn't say it out loud not to Ginny or Damien or Mathis. Not even to my own reflection in the mirror. But I was worried the next thing I'd be forced to give up would be sex. And once that was gone, what was I but a declining burden on the two of them?

Just go to the doctor's, Sam.

Funny, when had my internal voice started to sound like Alba?

I wished it was a simple fix. But human doctor's hadn't been able to fix me yet. Each visit fed Wrath as they suggested I be more active get more rest, drink more fucking water. Change my meds. Some people saw doctors or Healers as fixers. I knew better. We were a stopgap. Death would come for all of us eventually.

As a healer though, I knew the likelihood that there was a magic pill, that would help me reclaim the ground I'd lost, out there in the universe, especially with a host of neurological symptoms, was unlikely.

So once the medical community failed me, it was about magic. Giving up the life I'd begun to carve out for myself one piece at a time.

"Well this is fucking depressing," I said to no one. Dawn was beginning to break over the water. Screw it, I'd go to Ginny's and do some yoga. See if she made any progress on my inspections.

Quietly I got up and stumbled to the bathroom. My hair was a mess. I'd slept on it wet. I pulled it up into a half ponytail, half bun hot mess. After emptying my bladder I washed and tried to ignore the urge to watch the water run.

Shuffling to the bedroom I grabbed some elastic waist pants and tried to pull them up. They fell right off.

I'd been wearing dresses that could camouflage a world of sins. Mathis hadn't noticed when he'd massaged me. Or when we'd had sex. It couldn't be that bad, could it?

Again I tried to haul them up, rolling the waistband for a little more security. Gravity won.

So much weight my mother had lost. Until she looked like a skeleton covered with skin.

"Damn it." I tossed the pants to the floor. Damien the neatnik would have a fit, but better a discussion about my sloppy ways than our discussion from the night before.

I found a pair of drawstring sweats and yanked them up, securing the knot. I pulled on a sports bra that zipped in front and topped with a hoodie. It wasn't the most elegant outfit but it freaking fit.

I headed out to the living room, Wally and Wilma bouncing along in front of me, ready for their customary scoop of food and early morning walk. No sign of the guys.

They couldn't be far. There was no way they'd have left me sleeping. The front door was unlocked.

I pulled it open and spied the cougars. They were curled together into little C shapes. I let the screen door slam, expecting them to jump to alertness.

When they didn't, I frowned.

"Stay," I told Wally and Wilma before making my way out onto the deck.

I could feel it then, the magic that pulsed off them. This was no normal sleep. Damien and Mathis had been mystically mickyed.

With a cry, I fell to my knees. Damien was closer so I crawled to him and leaned down, laying my palms on his body. He wasn't dead. I'd seen him breathing. Besides, Mathis had told me that the shifters would revert to their human shape when they were seriously hurt or dying. I sent out a healing probe of pure white energy into his form. His heart and lungs were good. I detected no real damage. But he was under big time. More like sedation than a natural level of sleep.

I added more energy into his body, using it to sweep away the heavy sedation spell. There was something about it that was unlike any magic I'd encountered before.

Damien was waking up. I could see his eyes darting behind his lids, so I turned to Mathis. I was so focused on them that I didn't see it right away. On the side of the trailer, someone had written five words in what looked like blood.

Soon Sam. Your Secret Admirer.

CHAPTER 10
SAM

Mathis woke up with a snarl and a swipe of his big claws.

"Easy," I snapped, falling back onto my ass. "It's just me."

The dark-eyed cougar froze. His warning growl turned to a purr when recognition dawned and then he shifted into his human form.

"Sam? You know better than to get that close to one of us when we're sleeping shifted," he lectured.

I pointed to the message. He glanced over his shoulder, straightened up, and then swore.

Damien was having a harder time shaking off the drug. He made soft whimpering sounds his eyes darting back and forth behind closed lids. I was tempted to give him another nudge but didn't want to fight with Mathis about magic use. Instead, I stroked the white streak along his shoulder and made soft, comforting sounds.

Mathis stumbled inside for pants. He returned

moments later buttoning the fly of his jeans still shirtless and barefoot.

"Did you hear anything?" he snapped. "See anyone?"

I shook my head. "I thought you guys were just mad and decided to camp out here."

He put his hands on his hips. "Sam, nothing would keep us from you."

"But you were shifted."

He scowled and then rubbed the back of his head. "Damien had that feeling again. Like someone was watching us."

This was bad. What sort of creature could get the drop on two paranoid shifters with a mate to protect?

Damien groaned and shifted. Bloodshot blue eyes focused somewhere beyond my shoulder.

"You okay?" I whispered.

"My head is killing me," he groaned. "What the hell happened?"

"My secret admirer struck again," I petted his hair as much to soothe myself as to him.

He could have died. They both could have. I could have woken up and found their bodies.

A cold shiver ran through me. Whoever my secret admirer was, the being was...playing with us. A cat toying with a mouse. Letting us know that I could be taken at any time.

Mathis was on the phone. He'd moved down to the sand and was scrutinizing it. Looking for tracks, probably. "It's me. You and Ginny okay?" He explained what happened to his twin while I helped Damien sit up.

"Yeah, bring Ginny over here and we'll go out on patrol together." He hung up and then turned to face us.

"Should we evacuate the community?" I whispered.

There was no chance that either of them would leave. But our other friends didn't need to be targets for a lunatic.

"No," Damien rasped. "They won't go if you're in danger. And since you can't leave, they'll stick around."

"Let's get inside." Mathis hauled me to my feet first and handed me my walking stick. "I feel exposed out here."

He half carried half dragged Damien inside and set him on the couch then supervised the corgis doing whatever they needed to do. Just as he ushered my pets back in, Ginny and Eric arrived.

"I brought coffee," Ginny set her backpack on the table. "And Fran's on her way. She's going to help us whip up a batch of fuck-off oil."

"Excuse me?" I couldn't have heard that right.

"It's your basic banishing oil with a little extra kick. Hopefully, it will tag your stalker

right in the bean bag."

"At this point, I'll try anything." I watched as Ginny set out her French press coffee pot and started boiling water, adding grounds, and whipping heavy cream. There was comfort in wrapping my palms around the mug, breathing in the fresh rich aroma that told me that today, with this witch's potion in my system, anything was possible.

Damien and Mathis came up behind me. "A moment, Sam?"

"I'll wait outside with Eric." Ginny winked at me and then left us on our own.

I looked up at my guys, sending out the lightest sensory tendril of white magic. Mathis had shaken whatever that spell was off, no problem. Damien still looked rough.

"You guys all right to go out?" I asked. I'd trust their judgment no matter what my magical probe was telling me.

Mathis nodded. "I'm solid. Damien's a little shaky so he's going up to the B&B to help Jim wrangle contractors for you."

I shut my eyes, trying and failing, to hide my relief. "Okay. Ginny, Fran, and I will be up soon. We're working on a banishing spell."

"I'd rather catch whoever is behind this," Mathis growled low.

So would I but after last night I needed the two of them safe more than I craved answers. "You two could have been killed last night. And if this secret admirer wanted me there wouldn't have been anyone to stop it from taking me."

They both started to growl. At least they didn't argue. Instead, Damien cleared his throat and said, "We called John last night. He's looking for your father."

Shock replaced the growing anxiety in my system. "What? How?"

"Scouring the internet," Mathis said. "He'll probably text you throughout the day asking for details."

"I don't know anything." I shook my head. "My mother never got the chance to tell me anything."

Mathis gripped my shoulders. "Listen to me, Sam. This is the only possible lead we have into whatever is going on with you."

My heart thudded. "You didn't tell John that there's anything wrong?"

"No, firecracker." Damien gave me a tired smile. "We wouldn't have asked him, but we don't know anyone else who can follow cyber trails."

I released a shaky breath. "Good. I don't want him to worry. I wish you two weren't so worried."

"And I wish you were well," Mathis pulled me into a tight hug. "Eric's waiting. Plus, I hear Fran and Sally coming."

"Be safe," I told him and stroked his whiskered cheek.

Mathis left giving me a moment alone with Damien.

"Are you all right?" I asked. He might tell me something that he wouldn't say in front of Mathis.

He let out a long, slow, breath. "Not really. Whatever it was that we were dosed with hit me hard."

"I can try—" I reached out intending to lay hands on him for a quick healing boost, but he caught my wrists before I could touch his chest.

"No, firecracker. No more healing. Not unless it's life or death. I know I can't stop you then, so the best I can do is hope it doesn't come to that."

I curled my fingers down and nodded. "I'm just so worried about you."

"Same, love." He kissed my temple, before pressing his forehead to mine. "I can't lose you, Sam."

I wanted to tell him he wouldn't but that felt suspiciously like a lie. So I made no promises and held him close for another minute more.

Creating the fuck off banishing oil was…interesting. The gathered members of the coven debated the best ingredients to use as we sipped Ginny's delectable coffee.

"Sea salt," Fran advised. "This is white magic and you want a level of protection for those casting it."

"Black and red pepper flakes," Sally added. "Bring some heat to the message."

"Green onion, for banishing pests," Ginny advised. "And I have oregano dried from my garden. Local grown to ground the spell and protect from possible backlash."

"A bay leaf to set the intention on the target," Bea added. "Oh, and garlic too to ward off evil."

"It sounds like we're making a marinade more than a spell," I quipped.

All the witches turned to face me. It was Bea who said, "Honey child, what do you think cooking is? We nourish our souls and those of our loved ones at the same time we nourish our bodies."

Sally broke out a large bottle of olive oil. "Although for banishment it would be stronger if we could actually feed it to the person we're trying to banish."

"A fuck-off buffet?" I quipped.

There was a round of cackling laughter and then the coven got to work.

I pulled Fran aside when Ginny and Sally headed back to her place to collect the fresh herbs. "Is there anything else I can do to set a protection spell around this place?"

Fran thought for a moment. "I'm not sure what. Bea already set a very heavy barrier spell around all entrances to the convergence. If your secret admirer can get through that, there's not much else that will keep him or her out."

Not the news I'd hoped to hear. "How did your research go?"

Fran shook her head. "Nothing, as expected. Our archives hold no instance of anyone ever escaping from the convergence. We did find one thing of interest though. Our convergence is the only one that takes people."

"Really? I frowned. "What does that mean?"

The hedge witch shook her head. "I can only speculate that it has developed an appetite for magical blood."

The thought of that had chills running up and down my spine. "No one lived here before Alba, right?"

"Not that we know of." Fran put a hand on my shoulder. "Don't worry, Sam. Everything will work out. And hey, the good news is that Ginny and I convinced your inspector that he made a mistake, so you are back on schedule. The contractors should be up at the B&B right now."

"Thank you." It was odd. A few days ago I would have been over the moon at that sort of progress. But after Mathis and Damien had been attacked, I was more concerned with securing my loved ones than meeting the demon's deadline.

"Are you sure this won't mess with my magic?" I asked Ginny as she handed me the clear bottle and gave me instructions on how much of each ingredient I should add. "I can't afford to lose my white witch status."

She nodded abruptly. "Positive. Banishment is used against creatures who terrorize and otherwise damage your calm. You're not interfering with free will."

"And you have the moon on your side," Sally added. "Waning moons are best for protection-type spells, which is really all this is."

I added the oil to a measuring cup with a pouring spout. Added the salt, the black and red pepper, and then minced green onion while the others gave me advice.

"Whip it up really good." Bea made a rapid stirring motion with her hand. "As Bob Ross would say, beat the devil out of it."

I whipped until my arm grew tired and then Ginny handed me a wax pencil and a single dry bay leaf.

"Write the offender's name on the leaf, add it to the bottle, and then top it with the oil."

I wrote *my secret admirer* on the leaf, stuffed it inside the small glass bottle, and then scraped the contents of the measuring cup on top, making sure I got every fleck of pepper and bit of garlic, before shoving the cork in.

"Now what?" I looked around at the faces of my friends.

Fran was frowning. "I think it'll be more potent if it sits for a little bit."

"But the problem is acute," Bea insisted. "She should eat some now."

Everyone else agreed with that. There was half a loaf of Damien's French bread in the microwave to protect it from bugs. I sliced it up and we all took turns dipping it in the oil.

"In two days, do it again," Fran advised as she picked up crumbs from the table with her index finger. "Maybe pour the oil over a steak and have your shifters grill it up."

"Oh, and light a candle you anoint with the oil," Sally added. "Ambience as well as setting the intention. Black if you have any on hand."

I nodded and then held out my arms. "You ladies are the best friends a witch ever had."

I was engulfed in a group hug. These witches had my back, and I appreciated every one of them showing up for me in my time of need. Even Bea, who gave me grief half the time, had put herself out.

"Does that mean you'll join us for the full moon revel?" Ginny raised her brows.

The full moon was almost three weeks away. And suddenly, I was less concerned about how I would look cavorting naked by torchlight than if I would still be able to participate at all.

"I would love nothing more," I told her.

Mathis and Eric came across Mel and Javier, who was in his alligator aspect. They too had been patrolling the convergence, though they'd started at the far end by their bar.

"Anything?" Mathis shifted back long enough to ask.

Mel shifted from the wild horse aspect they favored for combing the beach. "Not so much as a whiff."

"It doesn't make any sense." Mathis put both his hands behind his head and turned in a circle. "The barrier spell is intact. I felt it any time we passed the boundary to the convergence."

Much like an electric fence, the charge from a magical barrier made all the small hairs on his neck go up. It would keep those who wished members of the community harm out while allowing mortals free passage.

"Do you think it could be a mortal?" Mel's train of thought must have been running along the same line as his.

"How could a mortal have gotten the drop on Damien and me? Even if we missed their scent, they would have made a racket approaching." Mathis turned and stared out at the crashing waves.

His eyebrows drew together as he stared at the lapping waves. "The barrier only covers the land."

"It has to," Mel said. "Salt breaks the magic. The sea and the inland waterway have always been our natural boundaries. We would detect anyone coming in by boat long before they were close enough to do any damage."

"Everyone who reported the feeling of being watched has a place near the ocean side of the community,"

Mathis added. "And when Damien was attacked the other night, he claimed he heard a splash."

Mel turned to look at Javier. "Some of your people?"

The alligator shook his head baring wicked teeth.

Mel looked back at Mathis. "No, reptile shifters tend to hang out in bayou country. It's easier for them to blend in there. Besides, we'd see tracks or something if it were shifters."

Witches would need a boat. Same with gremlins and goblins. Aquatic shifters were few and far between and much like Javier's people, they didn't spend much time outside of their preferred habitats. True shifters like Mel were very rare, one in a hundred million. And even Mel carried a scent in whatever form. Same with the fae or demons. The stink of brimstone would have told them all right away.

His instincts were screaming that whatever creature they were facing wasn't something he'd seen before. What had no scent or had such strong magic that it could disguise its scent from Damien's nose?

Mathis wasn't one to speculate but as he looked at the sea he wondered. What if there's another sort of supernatural creature out there? One that wanted his witch? His claws shot forth and his hands clenched at his sides as the thought surfaced.

Over my dead body.

CHAPTER 11
SAM

The banishing oil must have worked. There were no more gifts or messages from my secret admirer. The night after we'd mixed the oil, Damien had grilled steaks marinated in the concoction and added it to a bed of greens for me. We'd dined on the deck with the anointed fuck-off candle and then gone for a swim, the first of the season.

"It's too cold!" I cried when I waded in ankle-deep, leaning on my cane for balance. Still, something about the lapping water soothed me, almost like the element was petting me.

"I'll keep you warm, firecracker." Damien came up behind me but before he could wrap me in his arms, Mathis in cougar form pounced. His claws were retracted but the weight of the mountain lion took Damien down hard. He came up sputtering with a mouth full of saltwater and shifted. As a mountain lion, Damien was larger and he dunked the other shifter with one swipe of his massive paws.

I laughed and clapped like a child, enjoying watching them frolic in the surf. I felt better than I had in months. That night the three of us came together for long overdue wild wicked sex. The only kind possible with two shifters and a lusty witch.

Everything was back on track with the grand opening of the B&B as well. Ginny and Fran assured me that they'd only given the inspector and contractor a nudge to get everything settled. No souls would be tainted in the pursuit of keeping to a demon's timeline. My fridge was delivered, the windows replaced, the countertops installed all on time.

I heard from John a few times a day. Unsurprisingly he found very little regarding my birth father.

"Why am I looking for this again?" He asked me and Damien during our weekly chat.

"Medical stuff," I said, sinking my nails into Damien's thigh. He'd agreed not to tell John about the symptoms if they didn't get any worse. "It would be good to have for Emily, don't you think?"

"I'll keep digging." John promised.

"Remember our deal, Sam," Damien murmured as he kissed my neck.

I threaded my fingers through his. "You'll hold your tongue if I don't get worse. Got it."

His blue gaze turned molten. "Do you really want me to hold my tongue?"

Then he proceeded to show me exactly how skillful he was with that appendage.

Wonder of wonders, my symptoms stalled. No more drain on my energy. No dizzy spells or blackouts.

With much of the stress off I found my appetite returning. I didn't gain any weight but I didn't lose any more either. It seemed like I'd finally struck the balance I'd been hunting for my entire life. I enjoyed my job, relished my time with my friends, and gave myself over to my lovers completely. I sang for them every night, enjoying the reprieve and the way they relaxed their guards.

The community was still on high alert but there had been no further weirdness, no more sensations of being watched. More proof that my secret admirer had been banished.

I woke up one morning, warm in Damien's embrace. He was sleeping in and Mathis was on patrol with Eric. We'd decided it was safe to reopen the restaurant for the weekend crowd.

"You should put the banishing oil on the menu," I teased him.

"That wouldn't work. We want our customers to come back." He'd proceeded to tickle me and I shrieked with laughter, startling the corgis into a barking frenzy.

This is what perfect looks like. I thought as I sat on Ginny's deck in my customary chair, focusing on deep and even breaths. Happiness radiated from me like a sun.

But a shadow named Wrath lurked at the edge of my mind and planted seeds of fear. *It can never last.*

The Investor arrived two days before the grand opening. He studied the details and went over the specs with me as I showed the upgrades to the kitchen and bathrooms and the accessibility for disabled customers which was borderline unique in smaller inns and short-term stay places in our area.

He twirled his cane and then *thunked* it down on the hardwood floor and nodded. "Well done, Sam. I worried you weren't up to the challenge, but you've proved me wrong."

High praise from the demon. "I think that means you owe me a boon."

The demon narrowed his eyes at me. "Aren't I paying you enough?"

"That's compensation. Why not sweeten the pot? Happy employees don't leave you hanging when times get tough."

He narrowed his eyes. "Fine. What is it you seek?"

"The answers to five questions." I set forth the opening offer.

"One," he countered.

"Three," I haggled.

Those goat slitted eyes narrowed. "Two."

"Agreed." I stuck out a hand. "To a bargain well struck."

The demon wrapped his three-knuckled fingers around my hand, engulfing it in his hold. "A bargain well struck. Ask your questions, witch."

I swallowed thickly. "Why does this convergence consume supernatural beings?"

"Ah, always looking out for your people. Such a noble leader. Well, as you know a convergence is merely a place where ley lines intersect, and power gets trapped. That power can be tapped into, but beings have been lost in the pursuit of mining that energy.

Enough of them perished on this ground that this particular convergence grew used to the constant sacrifice. Now it demands tribute from all preternatural beings. It takes powerful beings as a matter of course. If you want to get out ahead of it, I'd recommend starting up the old ways of ritual sacrifice to appease it."

I made a face. "Um, no, we're not sacrificing virgins or goats or anything else. Next question. How could someone escape from the convergence after he's been taken?"

The demon looked almost bored by the question. "He wouldn't. Not alive anyhow. Are you referring to your energy vampire ex? Are the mortal authorities still hounding you? I can scared them off if it would make my grand opening easier."

"That won't be necessary." The police had informed me that DNA and dental records confirmed it really had been Robert Sinclair's body. Even with the trash bag wrapping and note to me though, they had no evidence that he'd been murdered and his autopsy reported he'd drowned. The body had been in the water long enough that they couldn't pinpoint an accurate time of death.

"You haven't heard anything of a Secret Admirer?" The older deputy, the one with the salt and pepper mustache had asked during my final interview.

"No."

"Do you have any idea why someone would have written your name on his body?"

"Robert drank, a lot. It made him violent and unpredictable. He could have written it himself, intending to harass me, and then drowned by accident."

As far as local law enforcement was concerned I was a middle aged woman, a former battered spouse with a chronic illness. I had no means, motive or opportunity.

They did call Mathis in, but whatever he said during his interview had been enough to have the investigation officially closed.

The demon steepled his three-knuckled fingers. "So, there's no escaping the convergence once taken. It will suck your very life force from you. But if one were clever, one might be able to retrieve the body by following ley lines in and out. The problem here is that the convergence is beneath the sandbar we stand on. So the procurer of the dead would have to be able to hold their breath for a *very* long time. Maybe twenty minutes and that is if they were fast swimmers who could locate what they were after immediately."

"But that's impossible." No one could hold their breath that long.

"Precisely. Now, introduce me to the staff here. I like to make an impression before the guests arrive."

Other than me, Mathis, and Eric, I'd hired a head housekeeper and her two daughters who would take charge of cleaning the rooms and the establishment. The cook was a soon-to-be CIA, graduate, a grandmother in her late fifties who was starting over in the Outer Banks after a rocky divorce. Damien and Sally would fill in with eggs, muffins, and coffee until she arrived with her freshly minted degree next month.

"I'm planning a little reception here tonight," the

demon told me and gave me a slow once-over. "Have one of your shifters dress you properly."

I stared down at my loose dress which I loved mostly because it had deep pockets for any of my witchy bits and bobs. "You're planning to adequately compensate me for this, correct?"

The demon smiled charmingly. "Don't I always?"

"Because I make you," I grumbled. Despite pretty much everything that came out of his mouth, the Investor was growing on me.

Sort of like a fungus.

"Damien's going to escort you," Mathis said through the bathroom door. "Eric and I have patrol tonight. Besides Damien the one with the pretty social skills."

"You'd be fine if you, you know, gave a fuck," I called back.

"My fucks are finite," Mathis drawled, demonstrating that hint of Texas that I hardly ever heard. "And given only to very special people."

I snorted and then put the big brush down. I hadn't let my shifters dress me as the demon suggested. Instead, I'd slipped into a silver dress I'd ordered for a special occasion a few months ago. My hair was loose in a wild riot of curls. I couldn't remember the last time I'd worn make-up. Probably Ginny and Eric's wedding.

Working every day in a construction zone didn't mix

with fancy dress. I stepped back and leaned on my cane so I could check out the back. It was flouncy and feminine but still sexy. And still unzipped. Once it was it would be a total ass-grabber. I didn't own a thong so I was going commando.

Doubt assailed me. Was it too much? The dress I'd worn to the wedding had been much less formal. Beach equaled casual. But it was too late to change if we were going to be on time.

"I'm coming out. Don't you dare laugh," I cautioned.

"Wouldn't dream of it, little witch."

Taking a deep breath for courage I yanked the door open and stomped into the room, lifting my chin, eyes flashing in challenge.

Mathis's lips parted. He scanned me from head to toe, taking his time. It was a slow perusal that I felt through the mating bond like a caress. I shivered and then turned, using my free hand to hold up my hair. "Would you mind?"

A proprietary purr filled the room and I blushed with satisfaction. *This is awesome.* I felt powerful and feminine even without any of my witchy materials or tapping my magic.

His fingers traced the line of my spine before reaching for the zipper. I closed my eyes, doing my level best not to sway into his touch as he drew the tiny pull up.

"Almost ready, firecracker?" Damien called from the other room.

"He's going to have a heart attack when he sees you in this," Mathis growled in my ear.

"Stop," I said though I loved the compliment, the pride he felt in me. Turning in his arms I asked, "Are you sure you won't change your mind and come with us?"

"Tempting as you are, I promised Eric." He tucked a stray curl behind my ear. "Besides, just because it's been quiet doesn't mean we can drop our guards."

"Who are you kidding, you never drop your guard." I added a wink and a playful grin so that he knew I was teasing.

Before I could blink he reached an arm out and wrapped it around my waist. His tone was soft as he murmured. "Only for you, Sam."

His lips feathered over mine in a soft hot promise. His finger traced the line of the zipper and an image appeared in my mind, a clear picture of him dragging the pull down and helping me out of the dress, his rough hands caressing the flesh he slowly exposed until I was naked and panting.

I was on the verge of saying to hell with the Investor, his soiree, and everything else and just dragging him to bed when he stepped back.

"Save that for later, love." He released me just as Damien rushed into the room. His feet were coated in sand and he wasn't paying any attention to either of us. "Your stupid dogs were being stubborn as usual and—" The tirade cut off as he took in the sight of me in the dress.

"You like?" Mathis's reaction had boosted my confidence, and I pivoted, leaning on my walking stick.

Damien's blue eyes turned hot.

"Like isn't a strong enough word," Mathis murmured

and then clapped Damien on the back. "Into the shower now. Don't you dare embarrass our mate." With a wink, he left.

Damien reached for me and then grimaced when he glanced down at his hands. "Five minutes, I promise."

While I was waiting, I poked through my jewelry box. It was an ornately carved one made out of driftwood. It had been Alba's. Tears pricked the corner of my eyes when I remembered Damien gifting it to me.

"She'd want you to have it." He said with a sad smile. "You were like a daughter to her."

Deciding I needed her spirit with me tonight I dug through the contents and then frowned when I spotted the enormous sapphire that had been given to me by the goblin queen. It was a token of regard as well as a promise of future help if I ever needed it. For a moment I considered if I should use it to ask about my secret admirer. But the urgency had gone. I wanted to hold it for a time when we really needed it.

Hopefully, a time in the very distant future.

"How do I look, firecracker?" Damien strode into the room, handsome and distinguished in a charcoal gray suit that set off the blue in his eyes and threads of silver at his temples.

I shut the jewelry box and turned to face him. "Let's get this show on the road."

CHAPTER 12
SAM

The party was in full swing by the time we drove up to the parking lot.

Damien sat for a moment, staring at the structure that he'd considered home for most of his adult life. "It looks so different."

"It's just paint." It was more than that though. Head high torches lined the gravel walkway from the parking area up to the porch, casting shadows as well as illuminating the path. The flower beds had been replanted and fresh mulch added. During Alba's time the B&B had been scruffy, but a haven for a witch or shifter in need of a safe place. It hadn't been much to look at and even after we'd cleaned out the hoard of magical items that had filled the poky rooms from floor to ceiling in some spots, it was still often cramped, the air stale with disuse. Staying at the B&B during Alba's time made a body want to get their shit together and leave.

Now *the Sawgrass* welcomed people, beckoning them to come in and spend their hard-earned money to stay for a spell. To linger over coffee and pastries and ease into their day.

"I miss the old place," I admitted. "It doesn't feel like our space any more, does it? The community's, I mean."

That had been the goal, the Investor said. Mortals had wealth and would spend freely if they were promised luxurious and unique accommodations. As the demon had sniffed, "The convergence might be a safe harbor for every ragtag supernatural entity out there, but the B&B doesn't have to be. We're not running a charity and people pay more for nicer digs."

Damien took my hand and brought it up to his lips. "You did a beautiful job though, firecracker. Alba would have been thrilled to see the old place like this."

I fervently hoped so. "Well, we might as well go in. The sooner we make nice, the sooner we can get out of here."

The silver dress shimmered under the torch light. On opening day I would be back in one of my floral knit garments, with pockets, and working the check-in desk. Ordering Eric and Mathis to escort the first guests to their rooms and fix whatever needed fixing. Tonight, the Investor had made it clear that my role was to greet the people he was trying to impress and talk about the renovations as well as oversee the catered meal Damien's restaurant had provided.

Laughter and the sound of glass clinking and champagne corks being popped drifted through the space. With so many walls down the space appeared grand, like something out of a bygone era. The recessed lighting had been turned down and candles stood in ornate candle holders. Not drippy fat pillars or votives like the coven used in spellcasting, but elegant tapers all the same cream color that added the faintest whiff of honeysuckle to the air.

"There you are!" The Investor waved us over. "There are some fellows here who were asking specifics about the renovations."

Damien escorted me over to the men. I'd forgone my walking stick for the evening. It didn't go with the dress. Instead, I carried a silver cane with a rubber tip which was much more discreet, even if it was less witchy. I offered a tight smile as we approached. Being stared at was not something I would ever get used to and the three of them stared so intently I wanted to snap.

A low growl rumbled deep in Damien's chest, though it couldn't be heard over the classical music pouring from the smart speakers.

"Easy," I breathed at him. "They don't mean anything by it."

He let out an audible breath, clearly not happy. Damien might be willing and even eager to share me with Mathis, but I was still his mate. No power in the universe could keep him from viewing other men as a threat. He was still my familiar though and if I thought he couldn't handle me making nice with the Investor's guests, I'd order him to the kitchen to oversee the catering. Hopefully that wouldn't be necessary.

"Samantha Sinclair, I'd like to introduce you to Wade Wolenczak and Caspian Summers." The Investor waved a hand at the two men dressed in expensive suits. Caspian was tall and fit with snowy white hair that made his blue eyes seem brighter. He was probably close to seventy but whatever he did to maintain his muscle tone, it worked for him.

"Ms. Sinclair," he greeted me. His accent was almost lyrical. I couldn't place it. "I was just admiring your handiwork. I've been here before you see. Many years ago. And the place has aged beautifully. You managed to capture so much of the original charm while bringing the place up to the modern standard."

"Thank you, Mr. Summers." I dipped my head accepting the compliment with grace. "The B&B has meant a lot to our family so it was really a labor of love."

"Is that so?" The other man, Wade, was closer to mine and Damien's age. His dark blond hair hid any strands of gray but there were deep lines around his gray eyes and mouth. Something about his smile unnerved me.

I did my best to bury my unease. "Yes, Damien's mother and father bought the place when he was young. He was raised here and it's where we first met. Now we hope our son and his family will be able to come and enjoy the place the same way we once did."

Damien's shoulders relaxed slightly as I talked about our long-term connection to the B&B. It had taken me awhile to understand that by telling other people about John and Emily as well as our history, the animal in him felt like it was being claimed by his mate. And that more than anything was the same message I was trying to send to Wade of the shifty eyes and sneaky smile.

He got the message too and if the way the muscle

jumped at his jaw was anything to go by, he didn't care for it. Why?

The Investor hooked his own cane over his arm and plucked three glasses of champagne off a passing tray. He passed one to each of his guests and the third to me. Damien had to snag one for himself and whatever ground I'd gained by claiming him that way was lost by the demon intentionally snubbing him.

"A toast then. To successful ventures and the attaining of long-term goals," The investor said.

"Cheers." I raised my glass and didn't miss the way both Mr. Summers and his companion were watching me or the way Damien studied them, far too intently.

It was probably a good thing Mathis hadn't come. His fuse was longer than Damien's but there were some things he didn't tolerate at all.

The bubbles tickled my nose as I took a sip from my champagne flute and then forced a smile as the Investor led the men off and called another group over to meet me. It was going to be a long night.

***

MATHIS RAN in his cougar form up and down the stretch of beach, hunting, scenting for any discrepancies. The combined scents of strangers and Sam's anxiety drifted to him. Through the familiar bond he felt her irritation. In his shifted aspect instinct screamed at him to find her and soothe her distress. Enough of the man was left that he knew that would only upset her more if he showed up to a fancy cocktail party as either a mountain lion or a naked man.

Although his mate would appreciate it in private.

He spotted his twin in the distance. Eric's thick tail swayed slowly back and forth. A sign that all was clear on his end of the perimeter. Nothing to do but head home then. They'd patrol again after the party broke up and once more just before dawn, their usual pattern. To make sure nothing changed overnight.

Mathis ducked his head and ran toward home. His instincts screamed that something was off, but he couldn't smell anything. He wanted to have faith in the coven's banishing potion, in Sam's magic, but those ingrained feelings of being hunted wouldn't quit. Eric had told him once that Mathis had more highly developed instincts than the rest of them combined.

"You can always sense when there's a threat. I don't know if that means you're paranoid or have a sixth sense that the rest of us don't. All I know is better you than me."

Skipping the stairs, Mathis leapt up onto the front porch, shifting as he went. He crouched as a man, letting the last tingles from the change wash through his cells. He'd had this ominous feeling a few times before. When he first realized that the pack they were part of wasn't as safe as they'd been led to believe. When Eric had been attacked by the other shifters and again when they'd been on the streets. When he'd learned about Damien's having a mate. And most recently, the day Sam had arrived.

He had that feeling again. Looming danger, inevitable change. But there was no scent, no source to point a finger at and say *there, there's the thing that's wrong. Let's kill it.*

The trailer door was unlocked. Sam and Damien knew he was out running shifted and had no way to carry a key or a cell phone. He opened the door, and scented the air, but there was only the faint trace of Sam's perfume and Damien's aftershave. No strangers.

After pulling on a pair of sweats, Mathis headed to the fridge. There was a whole roast chicken already cooked as well as a Tupperware full of rice and vegetables. He set the food on the counter and began fixing himself a plate. Once it was heating in the microwave, he went to the end table where his phone had been charging.

A text message sat waiting.

John Moss: *Found something. Call when you get this.*

Mathis dialed. John picked up on the first ring. "You're not going to believe this."

"Not going to believe what?" Mathis turned as the microwave dinged. "You found your grandfather?"

"Not exactly. My mother's mother disappeared for a summer when she was eighteen. She was on a road trip with friends after high school graduation. One morning they woke up and she was gone. No note, nothing. There was a search as well as several newspaper articles. After a month, the search died down because there were no leads, nothing for the police to follow. Her parents hired a private investigator but by then the trail was cold."

All the fine hairs were standing at the nape of his neck. "When did she show up?"

"Six months later they found her on the beach. Naked and pregnant."

"Where?" His heart was pounding.

"About a mile from the place where she disappeared." John swallowed. "That was several years before the Moss's bought the land. What does this mean?"

He had to tell Sam and Damien. Now. To hell with the party, this couldn't wait. "Thanks, John, I'll handle it."

He hung up and ignoring the food, headed to the bedroom. News like this was sure to send Sam into a tailspin. He should at least try to show up in decent dress so he didn't embarrass—

Movement in the corner of his eye. Mathis whirled, his teeth bared, claws shooting out.

The dart caught him in the arm and he crashed to the floor.

CHAPTER 13
SAM

We were halfway through dinner when a wave of panic swamped me. Caspian was talking about his own investments, a series of resort hotels to the south when his voice fuzzed out like a radio station losing a signal. I stared at him even as an overwhelming sense of dread flashed through my mind.

Then for a moment it was as though I was somewhere else. Trapped. Unable to get up, to free myself. My limbs were heavy and sluggish. Water lapped as I was dragged, helpless into the churning sea. It would swallow me whole....

"Samantha?" Wade touched my shoulder jolting me back to the present. "Are you well?"

"Fine," I croaked, pasting on what I hoped was a reassuring smile. "Forgive me, I just need the restroom for a minute."

My palms were sweating, and my heart thudded in my ribcage. The kitchen door swung in and Damien strode forward, his blue gaze going right to me. From his expression I felt sure he had experienced the same feelings that I had. "You felt it too?"

I grasped his arm like a lifeline as he murmured low enough for my ears alone, "What is it?"

"Mathis," I breathed. That had been his panic I'd sensed. "Call Eric and if you can't reach him, Ginny. Something must have happened when they were on patrol."

I sat at the check-in desk while Damien called. Eric answered right away and Damien switched to speaker.

"Patrol was standard, and neither of us saw or heard a thing. Mathis was heading home last time I saw him."

"Go check on him," I ordered at Eric. "We'll meet you there as soon as we can."

Damien met my gaze. I could tell a part of him wanted to bark commands and take control of the situation. He was dominant, had led the pack here for decades, but I was the Matriarch, the de facto pack leader. He would obey my instructions and hold his tongue.

The Investor appeared as though summoned, his gaze sliding from Damien to me and back." Is everything all right?"

"We're not sure," I told the demon. "We need to go investigate."

His gaze narrowed to slits. "I require you here."

I studied him for a long minute. "This isn't negotiable. A member of my pack might be in trouble." I turned toward the door, Damien holding my arm.

"If you leave now, Samantha Jean Sinclair, don't bother coming back."

I stopped shoulders tight. Damien was growling low in the back of his throat at the threat.

"Let's go, Damien." I didn't need the job and didn't want to devote my limited energy to the B&B if my boss was going to be a tool. No need to flounce out or make a scene. This place was no longer ours anyway. Tonight had driven that point home. Dealing with human tourists was probably more than I could stomach.

Damien helped me down the steps and then ran to get the Jeep. The Investor followed us out.

"Think this through, witch," he snarled. "You're the one who wanted to remain here."

I didn't look at him. Who knew what powers the demon possessed? I wasn't going to risk that he could compel me to do as he wished. "You're right, I did. But I've changed my mind." We had Damien's restaurant and a few of the trailers and cottages that belonged to the community for rental income. Plus *Mel's*. Like Damien said, we were Gen-Xers. We'd survive.

Damien pulled the Jeep to a stop in front of me and leapt over the side, the move too preternatural to be human. He held the door and the second my seatbelt clicked into place he slid back behind the wheel and sped down the black highway leaving the demon, the B&B, that part of our lives behind us.

"Did you feel it?" I asked him.

He shook his head. "All I sensed was your distress. Can you sense him, through the bond?"

My eyes slid shut and I felt my way down the golden

tether that linked my mind to my familiars. Damien throbbed with anxiety beside me but from Mathis, I felt... nothing. The thread that should have connected us had been severed.

I choked back a sob. "He's not there."

Damien's knuckles turned white where they gripped the steering wheel. "What do you mean?"

"The bond just dead ends." My body began to quake as I considered what that meant. "Damien, it's like he's—"

"Don't say it," Damien growled. "Don't, Sam."

I pressed my lips together and tried to hold back the tears.

Damien took the turn onto the beach fast and sand sprayed from the Jeep's tires. I couldn't think. My whole body had gone numb and for once, MS had nothing to do with it.

Ginny stood on the porch holding Wally and Wilma by their leashes. They yapped and strained to get to me, obviously sensing my distress.

"Eric's inside."

I barely heard her, focusing all my concentration on making it up the steps.

A plate sat on the table, the food still warm. Damien sniffed it first. "No trace of poison."

Poison?

He headed down the hall and returned with Eric, who had wrapped a bath towel around his hips. "I found this." He held up what looked like a dart.

Damien took it from him and held it beneath his nose. He drew in a deep breath and then shook his head. "Nothing. It's like the scent is camouflaged somehow."

"Mathis?" I asked Eric.

He shook his head. "There was no sign of a struggle. Nothing to suggest he had a chance to fight off attackers."

The walking stick that Mathis had carved for me stood by the door. I should have brought it. It was a talisman, a connection between the two of us. Dropping my cane I lunged for it, needing to feel the smooth polished wood that he'd painstakingly sanded and lacquered just for me. My left side went numb and my leg, the one supporting my weight, began to buckle. Damien dropped the dart and caught me before I landed face-first on the floor.

"Water," I gasped, recalling the panic.

"Get her a drink," Damien misunderstood as he swung me up in his arms.

I shook my head. "No, water. It was an image he sent me. He was panicked about the water. Woke up as someone was dragging him."

Damien's eyes went wide. "Eric, get Ginny to sit with Sam." He began toeing off his dress shoes and shucking his jacket as Eric disappeared onto the porch.

I reached for him as he yanked his shirttail from his trousers. "You need to be careful, Damien. I can't lose you too."

"Don't give up on him, firecracker." Damien paused long enough to hold my gaze. "Mathis is a fighter."

I clung to the cobweb of hope he dangled in front of me and wrapped it around myself. It was a thin thread, but better than the yawning despair that threatened to gobble me up.

Ginny came through the door the second Damien shifted. They passed one another and Ginny strode right to me, taking my icy hands in her warm ones.

"We need to call the coven," she told me. "Ivan has an Echoes Enchantment spell. It pulls memory from a space and allows us to see what happened. It takes a lot of power though, we need everyone here to use it."

I nodded. "Call them."

She picked up her phone and moved into the kitchen while I sat on the couch. Wally and Wilma jumped up beside me and I petted them absently. I had no idea how much time had passed when a naked Damien strode into the trailer. "There are drag marks and I caught Mathis's scent. You were right, the trail heads right into the sea."

And now our bond was severed. *Oh god, Mathis.*

Eric rushed in. "There's another note from your secret admirer. It's written in the sand."

My head turned to him but I didn't see him. They were identical and yet so different. *Mathis*, my heart cried his name.

My lips said, "Show me."

I'M COMING FOR YOU. *Your secret admirer.*

"Fucker," I snarled even as I clung to Damien's shoulders. "That sick bastard is going to pay."

I read the words that were written next to the dragline that indicated where my secret admirer had hauled Mathis into the water. He'd been aware but unable to fight. And the sick bastard had taken the time to write me a message. Almost as though he were making a vow.

"No scent?" I asked Eric.

"Only Mathis. And that disappears under the waves."

Bea had arrived and was waiting on the porch, her hair done up in curlers. She studied my face and then, to my surprise, reached out and patted my arm. She didn't speak as she proceeded into the trailer. Eric held Wally and Wilma on the porch.

The others were crammed into the kitchen and dining room. The lights were off, and candles had been lit. Jim held Sally's hand. Sally gripped Ginny's, and Ginny in turn held Fran's who held Ivan's. Bea stepped forward and gripped the Russian's palm and held out hers for me.

Damien strode forward but instead of setting me down, he lowered himself so I could close the connection between Bea and Jim while funneling his familiar power into me.

An image flickered in the light of one of the candles as Ivan fed his strength into the bond. Conjuring what looked like a shadow. It grew until it was human-sized, standing before the now-cold food on the table. Mathis, with the phone held to his ear. I saw his lips moving but couldn't hear what he was saying.

"Why is there no sound?" I asked.

Ivan shook his head. "This is not like a video playback recording. What we see is an echo of the person, an emotion that fuels the spell."

We watched the echo of Mathis pace. The hand that wasn't holding the phone kept clenching and unclenching. From the couch echoes of Wally and Wilma watched him with worried eyes. Suddenly, Mathis paused and then spun on a heel and stalked into the bedroom.

"What's happening?" Damien growled. "We can't see him."

"If we break contact the spell ends." Sweat beaded Ivan's forehead. I'd been the conduit for a few spells before and I guessed the strain the conjurer was under was depleting his reserves.

"Eric!" Damien snapped.

A moment later Eric and the corgis appeared. "Is it over?"

"The echo went into the bedroom. Go in there and report back."

Eric dropped the leashes and hurried into the bedroom. Wally and Wilma leapt onto the couch and unnervingly lay in the exact same spots where their echo selves resided.

"He's down. There's something here." Eric called.

"Put me down," I told Damien. Jim was swaying on his feet. We'd lose the spell in a moment. "You need to see whatever he's seeing."

Damien set me down and then hurried into the bedroom. Keeping one eye on our conjurer, I focused on the dogs. They were yappy little terrors at the best of times. So why hadn't they reacted to someone coming into our home to take Mathis?

My question was answered a moment later. I heard Eric curse and felt Damien's shock and frustration even before the words drifted down the hall.

"It can't be."

"What?" I cried. Dizziness washed over me and like the sensation I'd experienced at dinner, I was seeing through another's eyes. Through Damien's eyes.

He beheld a being made entirely out of water.

CHAPTER
FOURTEEN

No wonder there was never a scent to follow. Damien had watched the scene play out as the being made entirely from the ocean slid in around the cracks of the closed bedroom window.

"It's an elemental," Eric breathed.

Damien had heard tales of elementals before. According to legend they were creatures made entirely from the elements themselves. Water, fire, earth, or air that could move through the world without leaving footprints or scents behind. Unable to speak, elementals could touch and be felt and were often the benevolent forces in the stories that looked after the favored heroes and children. They were believed to be nothing more than myths.

The being came together and though it had no discernable features, it pointed at Mathis, who still was unaware of the danger. The elemental propelled a dart from its index finger. It struck Mathis in the arm and the echo shifter collapsed. The elemental surged forward and cast a net made of seaweed over the unconscious male. It dragged him to the window before laying a watery palm on the glass. The pane disintegrated into sand under the creatures' touch. The watery figure clambered over the sill, then dragged Mathis out behind it.

"It was closed when I came in," Eric breathed.

The elemental turned and with a wave of its hand, the sand rushed back together, reforming the oversized plate-glass window good as new.

"It has power over the water, the sandbar. Everything to do with the ocean or the land that touches it." Damien hissed.

He ran to the window and spied the thing dragging Mathis down to the shore. Not wanting to let it out of his sight Damien threw open the window and shifted to his cougar aspect, running after the echoes.

The being made from water dropped the net, turned to the sand, and began to write the message he and Eric had found. No expression, no emotion at all on its watery features. Damien's gaze fixed on the net, which began to twitch. He stalked closer and saw that Mathis's eyes were open. The shifter was coming to, shaking off the dart's poison. He'd been so close. In another moment he would have changed into his cougar aspect and used his claws to destroy the net that held him.

But then the elemental turned and picked up the tied end, its destination the waves ahead.

No! Damien's mind screamed. He charged forward to stop the being from dragging Mathis into the waves, from drowning him. There was nothing to stop. The elemental wasn't there. Neither was Mathis. The vision wavered and then the echoes vanished into nothingness.

This had already happened when he was fucking around in the kitchen of the B&B, Mathis was dying....

Damien threw his head back and screamed and screamed and screamed. Eric also shifted into his predator form and joined him. Their cries filled the night. Any humans would be sure to steer clear of this stretch of beach for the night. The helpless outpouring of grief and loss was swallowed by the endless uncaring sea that had taken one they loved. A member of their pack.

Sam

I SAGGED to the floor when I heard Damien's panther cry.

Through our connection, I'd seen it all. The thing. It had struck Mathis down and dragged him to a watery grave. A tear slid down my cheek. We couldn't even bury him.

I couldn't breathe. The air was being stolen from me the same way it had been from Mathis. Only I was above the water. It was my body that refused to accept the air.

"She's hyperventilating," a distant voice said. Jim's, I thought. "Someone get a paper bag."

What the fuck for? If I'd had any air I would have

asked what they thought a paper bag could do when Mathis was...when he was...

Memory swamped me, so vivid it was as though I'd been transported back in time. The look in his dark eyes after he'd pulled up the zipper on my dress. It dissipated as quickly as it had come. The heat that radiated from him had been extinguished. He couldn't be...dead.

The paper bag was placed over my nose and mouth. "Easy, Sam. Easy." Another voice. It was so caring. Fran, the black witch, was working a calming spell over me. Trying to ease my pain, my suffering, the yawning chasm of loss that had opened in my heart.

Mathis was gone. My mind wanted to fight it, my heart to refute it because how could he be...dead?

Hands pulled me from my slumped position and guided me toward the couch. I didn't pay attention to whose they were or the soft soothing sounds of the coven as they moved around in my periphery. I wasn't tracking. Time was happening to me, but I stood outside it, numbed by grief.

Eric appeared, naked, coated with sand, eyes red from crying. He sobbed, falling into Ginny's waiting arms. I watched him from my observation perch where time flowed past as he mourned. His protector. The brother that had given everything for the twin he loved.

Damien staggered in. He scanned the room and then headed for the cabinet where he kept a bottle of whiskey. Part of me wanted to laugh. Who the fuck drank whiskey at the beach? Damien Moss apparently.

He didn't bother with the glass, just tipped it up, the

intention clear. To rid himself of the scene he'd just witnessed.

A scene I'd never forget.

When he went to take another drink, Bea snatched the bottle out of his hands. "Fool boy. You still have a mate to care for. You don't have the luxury of getting stinking drunk." She followed that up by taking a swig herself and then passing the bottle to Ginny.

Damien's red-rimmed eyes met mine. His lip quivered and he stumbled across the room to fall to his knees before me.

"Forgive me, Sam."

Somehow, I managed to reach out a nerveless hand and put it on his head. A benediction. He didn't need forgiveness. I saw his shoulders begin to shake as sobs racked his big body.

More time passed. People continued to make noise, to move around our home. Our home. Would it ever feel like home without Mathis? Signs of him were everywhere. The library book he'd been reading, something to do with naval history, was on the end table. One of his hoodies hung on the back of a barstool. His keys, phone and wallet were all in the seashell dish by the door. I spied it all from my spot on the couch.

Damien stopped sobbing but knelt quietly before me. I observed it all like traffic passing by on a train. Just the background, nothing to do with me. Someone said my name. Trying to get my attention. Nothing but the droning on and on no different than the constant roar of the murderous ocean.

Mathis, I thought. *I need to get out of here.*

He would understand, he always understood me. If I closed my eyes I could almost hear his voice.

No, little witch. It's not safe for you out there.

I wanted to argue with him that it wasn't safe here, where water creatures could drag a strong predator into the ocean on a whim. But he wouldn't hear. Couldn't argue. Would never stubbornly hold his ground again. I shook my head. Too much. It was too much to take in. The loss...

More voices arguing. I felt no need to contribute or even pay attention. No need to say a word to them. The familiar bond. My link to Damien, was on lockdown because whatever I was feeling, it ran too deep for me to even identify. If I'd been able to feel anything it would be fear. Not from the water creature. I feared Wrath. She opened an eye when I'd felt Mathis's fear. And now she wanted one thing and one thing only.

Vengeance.

If I set her loose, no one would be left alive.

So I shoved her down deep and then addressed the room at large.

"Does anyone know," I croaked to the room that went utterly still. "How to find that water creature?"

So we can kill it. Wrath sighed and shut her eye once more, biding her time.

"It's called an elemental," Jim explained. "But it was just a legend. I don't know anyone who has ever seen one in person."

Mel and Javier had closed the bar and joined us. Mel nodded their head at Jim's words. "It explains why none of us could pick up a scent. And how it retrieved Sam's ex from the convergence. No need to hold your breath when you're made of seawater."

"But why is it targeting Sam?" Sally asked. "What does it want from her?"

Ivan still looked pale after that spell. The big Russian was seated on the couch beside me. He patted my shoulder gently. "It admires her. Damien and Eric saw it write that message."

"But how do we kill it?" I asked the room again.

"That's the thing," Fran said. "You can't kill it because technically, it isn't alive."

"But they have souls," Ivan told her. "At least according to legend."

"Nothing with a soul could have done that to my brother," Eric snarled.

Damien had risen and was staring out the window. "If we can't kill it, can we freeze it? Keep it from doing any more damage?"

"Maybe if it was made from fresh water," Ginny said. "But it came from the sea. The salty water. No one I know has enough power to freeze an ocean."

Several gazes slid to me to see how I would take this news.

I shut my eyes. "What stopped them in the stories?" I asked.

"In the stories Alba told me, elementals were innocuous, sometimes even benevolent," Damien said. "I never heard of one killing before. Or fixating on a mortal."

Our gazes met, locked.

Damien whispered, "We need to leave here."

I stared at him. "You know I can't leave."

His Adam's apple bobbed. "The thing said you're next. Go stay with John and Jessica, at least until we figure out a way to destroy or contain it."

Bea thumped her cane on the floor several times to get our attention. "That might not stop the creature. Who knows how far it can travel from the sea? And outside of the convergence, Sam can't wield her magic without risking herself. She's better off here where she can protect herself and she has us to watch her back."

Damien ran a hand through his already disheveled hair.

"We can't decide anything right now." I spoke to the room without looking at anyone directly. "We're all exhausted and grieving. Go home. Get some sleep. We'll reconvene in the morning."

There were murmurs of agreement and they shuffled out. I could hardly stand the tender sympathetic looks or the tight hug Eric gave me.

Damien took Wally and Wilma out while I used the restroom. I thought about asking Damien to help me remove the dress, but I had promised Mathis....

Again I saw his eyes as he helped zip me up. No. I couldn't take off the silver dress. Not yet.

Damien appeared as I was returning to the living room.

His brows drew together. "I thought you were tired."

"I can't sleep in there." Not without Mathis. Not where he'd been taken.

Damien nodded in understanding. "I'm going to shift and keep watch."

I didn't have it in me to argue. Instead, I resettled on the couch. Wally and Wilma leapt up and circled half a dozen times each before claiming cushions. One by my head, the other draped over my feet. Damien flicked off the overhead lights and then disappeared into the bathroom, though he left the door open.

Several moments later the cougar stalked out. The big cat made the living room feel small. He sprawled on his side in front of the door, bodily blocking me from whatever lurked the night.

I stared at the gas log fireplace, cold and empty. Just like that thing out there, the elemental. There had been no pride or satisfaction in its watery eyes. No expression at all. It was tormenting me for no reason. It had taken Mathis, drowned Mathis, without even a moment's hesitation. The numbness surrounding my heart was ebbing. An elemental had fixated on me. Had retrieved the body of my abusive husband. Had murdered my lover. What did it hope to gain?

The coven didn't have any answers. I'd burned my bridge tonight with the demon. But I still had a resource, someone I could ask.

Slowly I sat up. Wally and Wilma lifted their heads, button eyes glinting. I leaned on my walking stick and tromped into the bedroom. Damien prowled silently behind me as I made my way to my jewelry box, lifted the lid, and fished out the sapphire.

"I'm going to go down to the shore," I said to him. "And don't tell me that it isn't safe. Nothing is and we need help."

His head dipped once in acknowledgment.

We made our way out the front door. The sand between the trailer and the ocean was too arduous for me to navigate on foot. Damien brushed up against my skirts before he lay sphinxlike on the sand, offering to be my ride. I climbed on his back, walking stick in one hand, sapphire in the other. The wind tugged at the silver silk of my dress as the big cat sprang up and surged toward the churning sea.

When he stood up to his elbows in the water, he stilled. Still perched atop him, I let my feet dangle down until the cold water lapped at the hem of my dress. I bounced the precious stone once, twice, three times in my hand and then threw it as hard as I could into the ocean.

Now there was nothing to do but wait.

CHAPTER 15
SAM

Heart in my throat I watched and waited. There had been no spell, no incantation or anything beyond throw the stone into a body of water. Would the goblin queen get my message? How long would it take her to come find me?

The wind lifted my hair and tugged at my skirts. I shivered.

Damien retreated until he stood above the waterline. I climbed off him and sank my toes into the cool sand, leaning heavily on my walking stick. Doubt assailed me. What if this didn't work? What if my last hope panned out to be worthless? Then what would I do?

No, this must work. I'd just tossed a giant sapphire into the sea. A sacrifice had been made. That was how magic worked, ebb and flow, give and take.

"What is it you, seek, energy witch?"

I started at the sound of the husky feminine voice. Damien lifted his head, whiskers twitching. There was no sign of anyone anywhere near us.

"Hello?"

"Over here." The voice came from a small tidepool a few feet to my left.

Leaning heavily on my walking stick I made my way to a tidepool illuminated by the last sliver of the crescent moon. Instead of my own reflection, the image of the goblin queen stared back at me. Eyes and skin dark as the night sky, hair white as fresh snow done up in a riot of elaborate braids. The goblin queen fit my mental image of an Amazon warrior, tall, thick, and heavily muscled. She wore a leather breastplate and tight leather pants and I could see the hilt of a sword jutting up over her right shoulder.

I fell to my knees. "Thank you for coming."

She inclined her head. "What is it you require of us?"

"Information, if you have it." I swallowed. "One of my mates was murdered by an elemental. A spirit of the water."

Her heavy brows drew together. "That is not possible."

"It happened. We saw the echo." I stroked Damien's head. "The creature has been stalking me."

Her forbidding countenance turned even grimmer. "Elementals do not concern themselves with the affairs of mortals, or even supernaturals. They are guardians of their assigned realm. They are rare to see as they have no use for humanoid shapes. They do not stalk and kill unless..." Her gaze grew distant.

"Unless what?" I leaned closer and would have fallen in the tide pool if Damien hadn't sunk his teeth into my skirt.

"It is rumored that elementals can be captured and forced to do the bidding of another. This would take more power than any land walker possesses though. Even a dozen covens of witches of your strength could not hold one of them."

Something about her phrasing drew me up short. "You said land walker. What does that mean?"

Her dark irises glittered. "You know that life evolved in the seas first before creatures slithered onto land to make it their new home. All that adapting greatly reduced their innate gifts. Those that were left behind have concentrated amounts of magic, much as sea snakes are far deadlier than their land-dwelling counterparts."

My lips parted. "Are you saying there are magical creatures living in the ocean?"

A nod. "They keep to themselves, wanting nothing to do with mortals or any of the magical community. It makes no sense that such beings would ensnare an elemental or have any interest in you or harming your mate though."

My throat had gone dry. "How do I communicate with them? Get them to stop sending the elemental to hurt us?" *How do I make them pay for Mathis?*

"You can't, at least not from land."

My gaze traveled to the white foam floating in on the rising tide. "So I have to go to them?"

The goblin queen nodded. "Yes. I can give you the means to travel to the dark heart of the ocean. Will this fulfill my vow to you?"

"It will."

"Look for it at high tide beneath the dark of the moon then." The goblin queen nodded. "And good luck, energy witch. You will most certainly need it."

Damien paced in front of the bathroom door. "Let me go."

"You can't," Sam said around her mouth full of toothpaste. "You know it must be me. I can't evacuate with the community. You can."

"But going into the ocean, to contact previously uncontacted creatures?" He shook his head.

She spat and then replaced her toothbrush in the holder. It sat beside his and Mathis's. A lump formed in his throat as he stared at them. All that would be left behind.

Her blue eyes were bright. She hadn't cried yet and he didn't wish to bring it up. "Damien, I need you to stay here, to do what you've always done. Look out for this community." Sam put her hand on his chest.

He stared down at her eyes which had the spark of life once more. "What are you going to do?"

"Find whoever sent the elemental," she said.

Heart in his throat he asked, "And then?"

A flicker of something dark moved in the shadows of her face. "Make them pay."

He studied her, his witch leaning heavily on her walking stick, still dressed in a silver ballgown. "Are you sure you're up to this?"

Samantha of a year ago would have been offended by the question. She would have gotten her back up that he even dared to ask. Then she would have brazened her way through, showing no sign of weakness. It demonstrated how much she'd grown to trust him that she took the time to consider his words and assess her own condition.

His gaze fell on her dress, specifically the hemline ruined by water and sand. "Do you want me to help you take that off?"

She swallowed and shook her head. "I'm not ready yet."

The hollow spot in his chest throbbed like an open wound. "Does this have something to do with Mathis?"

Her lip trembled and she glanced away.

"I know, Sam." Damien pulled her against him. "I loved him too."

When she met his eyes hers were lined with silver. "Did you ever tell him that?"

Damien nodded and a tear slid down her pale cheek even as she smiled. "I'm glad you did. I'm glad you two had each other before. He needed to be loved so badly—"

Her voice broke at the same time Damien felt his heart crack. It was too soon, but she needed comfort they both did. Scooping her up into his arms he carried her toward the bed. They had hours yet until high tide. He could either spend them arguing with her and in the end, she would order him to stay behind. Or he could make love to her and revel in the gifts they'd been given.

No matter how temporary.

He lifted her ruined skirts until he could duck underneath them.

"Damien, what?" she asked through her tears.

His claws emerged. He traced them gently up her thighs. "Say no if you want me to stop."

Sam

Did I want him to stop? Maybe I should. Maybe we both needed to hold each other and cry. But much like taking off the dress, that would mean letting go of Mathis. And I couldn't do that, not yet.

Hell no, I didn't want him to stop. Not now. Not ever.

So again dear reader we come to the point where if you aren't on board with the nookie, you need to skip to the next chapter and meet up with me there. Because I'm about to have some goodbye sex with my mate.

I couldn't see him, trapped as he was under the dress, but I could feel the scrape of his whiskers, the softness of his lips as he suckled the tender flesh of my inner thigh. "Please, Damien," I begged. "I need you."

He kissed and caressed me until I trembled. His hot breath fell on my delicate flesh. And just when I didn't think I could handle any more his rough tongue curved out and licked along my seam. A gasp escaped from between parted lips and I arched into him, needing to feel him deeper. Again he licked me, this time using his thumbs to spread me wider. The rough feel of his tongue as it glided over my wet flesh, prodded at my core, sought more of my wetness, made me moan. Gods, I loved him, this shifter. Loved the way he made me feel. And breathlessly I told him so.

He latched on to my clit with sharp teeth and purred even as one knuckle breached my core. The vibration made me come apart, flying to bits and pieces. He growled, a sound of pure masculine satisfaction, and began licking my orgasm from my center. He drew the pleasure out, making me crave him deep within, where the ache was growing.

"Enough," I gasped when he seemed fully intent to keep going. "Damien, I need you inside me."

There was a rending sound, as he fought his way free from my skirt. His face was cherry red, his blue eyes glittering as he shoved the athletic pants he'd been wearing since our return from the beach over his hips. He urged me over until I rolled to my side, skirts bunched high around my waist like some soon-to-be debauched Elizabethan lady. He curled up behind me and shoved one of his knees beneath my leg, splitting me wide. His hardness met my wet center and he rocked gently into me even as he kissed my shoulder. I pushed back into him, needing him to fill me up all the way. To take me rougher. To mark me.

He growled and his teeth bit into my neck.

We'd had playful sex before. And sweet, hot lovemaking but something about this joining was different. Primal. Life-affirming. This was fucking one's mate. The two of us stripped down to our base selves, giving in to our urges. A reunion with one another, a way to share our grief.

My nails sank into his arm as he moved inside me and the tears that had been threatening spilled over.

"I love you," I whispered even as a new release built within me. "I haven't told you that enough."

He was beyond words so he answered with action. Hauling me back deeper into his driving thrusts, using his fingers to seek out my clit beneath the skirt and drive me up over the edge.

I cried out as my body clenched him tighter, deeper, demanding that he gave me everything he had. With a snarl he did, plunging in as far as he could go, giving me everything he had, everything he could. Damien Moss, my mate.

I sagged into the mattress, sobbing. Not just for Mathis but for Damien too. Would I lose them both in one night?

His hot breaths fell across my bare shoulders and he kissed me. I felt the wet drops as his own tears fell.

Neither of us told the other that it would be all right. Neither of us believed it.

"Don't go," he whispered at one point, pulling me back against him. He was still in me, his shaft soft and tender. It wasn't sexual, not really. It was a plea. Him asking me if he could be enough.

"You are," I turned my face so I could look him in the eye. "You always have been. And that's why I must go."

Better for me to go on my own power than wait to be

taken by the elemental. To see Damien die too, trying to protect me from an unstoppable foe.

He rubbed a curl of my hair between his thumb and forefinger. "My Sam. At least this way you have a chance."

I swallowed but couldn't speak.

He sighed and then squeezed me tighter. "I love you, Samantha Sinclair."

I knew he did. "And you'll take care of them all for me?"

"Always," he breathed. "Sleep, firecracker. The new moon will rise soon."

And then I would leave him behind once again.

"If there were any other way," I told him. "If I knew that thing wouldn't come back.... Damien, I couldn't survive if I lost you too."

He swallowed audibly and rested his chin on top of my head. "And you think I can?"

I shook my head. "You need to. One of us needs to, for John and Emily. I might be fading anyway. You're the smart choice. The one they can all count on. You always have been."

He laughed but there was no amusement in it. "What does being the smart choice get me?"

"My heart," I told him. "I'm leaving it here with you."

There was nothing else to say after that. I sank against him and let tomorrow's worries drift off.

They'd find me again soon enough.

CHAPTER 16
SAM

When I opened my eyes my first thought was that it had all been a dream. That lasted until I woke in my tattered silver dress. Sand littered the bedding and fell to the floor as I got up and stumbled into the bathroom. My body ached and my head pounded. I stared for a long time at my reflection in the mirror. Thought about changing. If I'd been going anywhere else, I would have bit the bullet and taken the dress off.

But I was going into the ocean. Did it really matter what I fucking wore?

Distantly it occurred to me that I had no idea what the goblin queen was going to give me. A wetsuit? A submersible vehicle? It didn't really matter though. What mattered was that I had something to do, somewhere to go where I could let Wrath take over. Aim her at a target and give in. It would be like detonating an atomic blast underground and hoping that nothing would blow back onto the world above.

After brushing my teeth and washing my face I pulled my hair into a ponytail. My gaze traveled over the items on the counter. Cosmetics and pills and personal hygiene items. Damien, the neatnik, kept all his stuff in a drawer. Mathis and I were out of sight out of mind creatures. His razor, shaving cream, deodorant and comb were mingled with my hairbrush, clips, moisturizer and ponytail holders.

I left everything where it was. There was no sense packing for a one-way trip.

Wally and Wilma skulked behind me as I made my way down the hall to the kitchen. My corgis knew something was up. The coffee sat full and waiting, the rich aroma of French roast filling the air. I could just imagine Damien getting up at first light the way he always did and going through the motions of brewing a pot of java, knowing I was going to be a megabitch until I had my first cup of the magic bean potion.

The door opened and I turned to face Eric and Ginny, both of whom stared at me with wide, questioning eyes.

"I'm going with you," Eric announced. "We both are."

"No." I looked to Ginny who's lip trembled. "Damien needs you here to safeguard the community."

"No. Damien and Mathis both need me to safeguard their mate," Eric snapped.

"Mathis doesn't need anything anymore. He's—" I bit the word off, my lip trembling.

"We know you're planning a one-way trip, Sam," Ginny said. "And we want to come with you, to remind you that you're loved and needed here."

I shut my eyes. "You don't understand. I have no idea what the goblin queen is doing for me or if it will even work."

"All the more reason to have backup." Eric folded his arms over his chest and glowered at me. "Do you really think my brother would want you to go out in a blaze of glory to avenge him?"

"No," I said softly. "But he also wouldn't want me to risk your lives unnecessarily."

"Sam," Ginny moved forward and put out her hands. "Sam, you can't ask us to stay behind. You aren't well and if anything happens to you it will torment us both. Damien agreed to this already. I know he'd rather go himself but he's accepted that he needs to stay here. We don't. Please, don't fight us on this."

I looked out the window, to where the waves lapped the shore. The tide was out now, but by the time the dark moon rose, it would be back again, swallowing the sand.

"A cougar underwater?" I asked Eric.

He shrugged. "Unlike Mathis or Damien, my primary instinct isn't to shift when threatened. I can stay human. I can carry you if you need it. And Ginny is an encyclopedia of spells."

"Fine," I snarled. "Have it your way."

"Oh, we will." Eric winked the eye I'd given him back and then turned to talk preparations with Ginny.

I sat on the couch and Wally and Wilma jumped up beside me. I petted them both and tried to lock Wrath back down. She wasn't happy but with Ginny and Eric in the blast zone, I had no choice.

You can't ignore me forever, Wrath hissed. *Soon I won't give you a choice.*

WE SPENT the afternoon prepping as best we could. Ginny, Eric, and I each carried a hiking backpack complete with fresh water, protein bars to last us for a week, and a change of clothing. Eric packed extra food and water while Ginny and I debated what magical items we ought to bring. The saltwater complicated matters as salt was for the protection of the witch who was casting as well as being in the elemental's wheelhouse.

In the end, we decided a few gemstones each sewn into our pockets would help amplify our natural abilities. Ginny packed dry herbs, a scrying mirror, and chalk. I packed Alba's grimoire, my black hilted athame, and a small ceramic mortar and pestle. And a vial of dirt from Alba Moss's grave.

Though the days were getting longer, the sun sank behind the trees a little after five that evening. The entire community had gathered on the beach at high tide to see us off. My lips parted and what came out wasn't something I planned. The words to *Every Rose Has Its Thorn* escaped and carried on the wind. Damien took my hand as I sang the mournful rock ballad for Mathis as well as bidding the community a silent goodbye.

The light had passed beyond the horizon by the time the final note was swept from my lips. Something glittered to the east, beneath the waves. At first, it looked like a phosphorescent trail snaking through the water. Then something breached the surface. Round and smooth it moved toward where we waited on the beach, so bright it was like looking at an aquatic version of the Northern Lights.

"A submarine," Damien breathed as he squeezed my hand.

The thing was more than a sub though. It rolled forward and I spotted heavy treads like a tank beneath its bulk.

The hatch opened more like a UFO than a sub. A ramp lowered and we got our first glimpse of the interior.

"What's it made out of?" Sally whispered. "It looks...alive."

She wasn't wrong. The way the light pulsed looked like an overgrown firefly. I stepped forward and placed my hand on the exterior. It was firm, but warm, almost like a living being. The flashing pattern sped up under my touch and a smile stole across my lips.

"I think...it's alive."

"It can't be," Damien grated. "It's a machine."

There was an odd chirping sort of sound as though the submersible was arguing with him.

"There's no one driving." Mel had scrambled up the ramp and was peering within. "It must be a biomechanoid. Part beast of burden, part tech. Did anyone know the goblins could craft something like this?"

No one answered. We hadn't. And because it was the

only way for us to get where we needed to go, we didn't want to ask too many questions, either. I smoothed my hand along the hull and then turned to face Damien.

"I hate this," he whispered.

"I know."

He cupped my face in hands that shook. "I know you can't promise anything, but if you can, come back to me."

I shut my eyes and nodded. "Take care of my dogs. I know they're spoiled and obnoxious but I love them."

"Anything for you, firecracker." His blue eyes glistened with tears and he bent down to kiss me. His tongue swept into my mouth, laying his claim. I accepted it greedily. My heart thudded and my nails sank into his forearms as I gave in to the urge to mark him a final time in any way I could.

He pulled back and pressed his forehead to mine. "I feel cheated."

My throat was clogged with emotion as I nodded my agreement. I couldn't stay, we both knew it. Last time he'd driven me away for my own good because I hadn't known about what he was or the danger of staying within the convergence. He'd been protecting me.

Now it was my turn to protect him and everyone we loved. And to get vengeance for Mathis.

"I'm not good with words," I murmured. "But you know how I feel."

"I do, love," he breathed.

Another chirp from the submersible, almost as though it was urging us to hurry. Leaning heavily on my cane, I stepped back. Ginny and Eric fell in behind me as I moved up the ramp and into the living submarine.

Once Ginny was inside, the door hissed. I raised one hand in a final farewell to our friends on the beach. They waved back, some with tears in their eyes. Damien's were spilling freely down his face. Mel and Javier flanked him, shifters showing support for their packmate. I had to turn away and distracted myself by taking in the ship.

It was seamless in design. No seats or seatbelts. The consoles jetted out from the walls at points and looked to be made from the same softly glowing material as the outer hull.

"So, here's a question," Eric muttered. "How do we navigate?"

No sooner had the words escaped his mouth than the submersible responded. A sort of joystick controller grew out of one of the consoles at the same time as the walls turned transparent, providing us a 360 view of the world around us.

"Thank you," I said and then frowned. "Um, any idea what we should call this thing? I don't want to address it as "Hey you," or "Greenie Meanie."

"Blinky?" Ginny suggested and Eric snickered. The sub trilled in what I interpreted as a happy sound.

"Blinky it is." Leaning on my walking stick I moved to the console with the joystick. There were a series of characters written on the screen before me.

"Hey Gin, do you have a translation spell on hand?" I asked, "I don't know how to read goblin."

"Hang on." Ginny dug through her backpack and came up with a pair of readers, the cheap kind sold at the drugstore. I frowned, but when I put them on and glanced back at the console, the writing appeared to be in English.

"I thought these might come in handy. They showed up with one of the fairy hoards and Alba gave them to me." Ginny passed a pair to Eric and then donned the final ones herself.

Distantly I wondered if Alba had foreseen the need for us to read goblinese.

One of the gauges was labeled hull pressure. Another, oxygen levels. Both were in the bright green zone. The joystick had compass-like arrows but no words.

"Blinky," I said. "Could you give us a place to sit, please?"

A chirring whine and then three high-backed chairs rose out of the floor side by side.

"Thanks," I said and sat behind the joystick. "Everybody good?"

"Yes." Ginny took the seat beside me, before the oxygen panel.

"Let's do this," Eric said and tapped at the hull pressure light.

"Ivan conjured us a trailing spell. All we need to do is invoke it." I told them. I unfolded a piece of paper and handed it to Ginny.

She read it once and then handed it back to me so we could read it together.

"Let us find what has been hidden. Let us follow the footsteps of the one who we seek."

Up ahead and to the right a white light blazed to life. The path the elemental had taken, it must be because it stretched from our trailer and disappeared into the water.

I PUSHED the joystick to the right, to the east, and Blinky rolled toward the trail. Sand churned beneath the treads as we headed down to the water. Within a moment the sea lapped at the viewscreen, leaving salty droplets on Blinky's exterior. Another churring noise as we hit the outer edge of the sandbar and then we were completely submerged.

IF NOT FOR Blinky's bioluminescence and the shimmering trail that we followed, we would have been traveling through the dark. Tiny organisms floated through the water like dust motes in a sunbeam, looking for something to attach themselves to. Ghostly images emerged from the dark high-lit by the green lights, corals, and plants covering objects that protruded from the sandy ocean floor before they were swallowed by the dark again.

"Shipwrecks," Ginny murmured. "The coast around the Outer Banks is lousy with them."

"That's why they call it the graveyard of the Atlantic," Eric added.

What looked like a torn sail appeared, billowing slowly as though beckoning blinky forward. I eased the joystick a little to the south to avoid it. We crawled through disintegrating debris of a shrimp trawler, upsetting a large eel that had made the wreck home.

More random debris, everything from fishing nets and discarded coolers mingled with sand and kelp. Blinky took it all like a champ, chugging steadily onward down the slope. Schools of fish split before us, their bellies flashing iridescently in the green and white magical light.

Time passed slowly, with nothing to mark it. Our phones had stopped working soon after we'd been fully submerged. The terrain smoothed out with fewer things getting crushed beneath Blinky's treads.

"I keep expecting my ears to pop," Eric muttered.

The pressure reading hadn't changed, though a new gauge had sprouted up next to it, reading fathoms.

"How deep is a fathom?" I asked. That was the sort of thing Damien would have known.

Ginny frowned. "If memory serves, 6 feet."

"Okay, so this is saying we're about 39 fathoms deep." How deep would we have to go to find sea people? Were we even in the neighborhood?

"We must be near the break," Eric mused. "I've been out here a few times, fishing with Damien. And Mathis." The last was said in a whisper.

I shut my eyes. For the first few miles, I'd feared we would come across Mathis's body trapped in that seaweed net. But there had been only fish and the disintegrating bones of ships.

"Sam, look!" Ginny gripped my arm and pointed to

the south where the magic trail curved around something. "See if you can get closer to that."

Obligingly I pushed the joystick south. Another wreck appeared out of the gloom like a horror story monster. Blinky's lights caught on what looked like an old-fashioned stove. This was a much older and larger vessel than the wrecks we'd seen before.

"Holy hell," Eric breathed. "I think that's the USS Monitor. At least what's left of her."

I stared out the window, remembered Mathis telling me about that ship that was lost during the Civil War. "Didn't they recover most of it?"

Eric obviously shared the fascination with Naval history with his twin. "The anchor, the gun turret, some other stuff. The wreck was too disintegrated to move by the time mortals had the technology to dive this deep."

Ginny nodded. "Plus, it's become a habitat for sea creatures—"

I gasped as a bright amber glow emerged from what looked like the doorway of light in the artificial reef. "Look!"

A *figure* appeared in the doorway. Backlit by the glow, it was impossible to make out individual features, but the being was tall with broad shoulders. A ray glided past, adding to the preternatural quality of the scene.

My hands clenched into fists. Was that an elemental? No, the glow of Ivan's trail was behind us. This was a different light. A different elemental?

"Is it...pointing?" Eric asked.

"I think so." I maneuvered Blinky's joystick in the direction being indicated.

And gasped. A whirlpool swirled behind us. At its center I could see something on the other side, but the water frothed and foamed too fast to make out its shape. The white trail fed right into the center though.

I looked at Ginny and Eric. They both gave me a singular nod.

"Here' goes everything," I muttered and pushed the joystick forward.

CHAPTER
SEVENTEEN

Mathis awoke in his cougar form shrouded in darkness. What the hell had happened? The last thing he remembered was talking to John about Sam's mother's abduction. He'd gone into the bedroom and then....

A snarl ripped out of him. The dart. It had paralyzed him so he couldn't move, couldn't fight, or flee from the being made of water. An elemental. He'd been frantic as it dragged him down the beach toward the water's edge. He remembered the wetness seeping into his clothes, the panic as it went over his head. And then what? He couldn't remember.

Was he dead? Somehow he doubted he'd be this sore if he had drowned. His body ached as though he'd been dragged behind a vehicle for miles. He lifted his head and sniffed. No scent of anything other than the briny ocean water. No light penetrated the space. He could see nothing, hear nothing.

Instinct took over. He reached for the familiar bond

first. It was...gone. Frantic, he scrabbled for the pack bonds and found those too had been severed. As though he had never been part of a pack. Had the elemental done this somehow?

He shifted, wanting the sensitive human skin to detect anything that his cougar might have missed. On hands and knees, he took in his surroundings. The floor beneath him was firm but pliable. He reached out his left hand and pressed and scrabbled in the dimness, feeling for a wall or bars. His fingers penetrated...water?

Sudden light flared from all around. He hissed and threw his arm over his eyes. His too-keen senses pained him at the sudden influx of illumination.

"You're awake." The voice was light and melodious.

"Where am I?" Mathis growled. "What is this place?"

"Our laboratory." The voice, it was female, answered easily. "I'm afraid we have to keep you contained, but I promise if you cooperate, we'll do our best to make sure you're comfortable here."

Laboratory? That didn't sound ideal. His pupils had shrunk and he chanced a glance over his arm, taking in the figure who had appeared with the light.

Her long red-gold hair tumbled over her shoulders in lustrous waves. Her eyes were a murky light gray color like an overcast August sky. She wore a white gown that looked a nightgown. If nightgowns were made out of bubble wrap. And the way she smiled at him made his skin crawl.

He took a moment to view the newly illuminated space. He was in some sort of bubble. Surrounded by water in all directions. Beneath his knees, the water faded into more of that inky blackness. No escape because the space he occupied was the only one where he could draw breath.

"Who are you?" he asked. "Why have I been brought here?"

"Greetings, Mathis Dracos." Her head tilted to the side in a distinctly birdlike manner.

"I had our guardian bring you to us. I am to be your mate."

His stomach lurched but he evinced no reaction as he informed her. "Sorry, lady. I already have a mate."

She bent down to touch the floor. As she drew her hand up, water followed forming a bench.

No, not a bench, he realized as the water spread farther out. More of a platform. Kind of like a bed.

The female who had yet to give him her name, sauntered toward it with an easy grace. As she went she untied the knot on one shoulder, making the garment droop precariously low on the right.

"You're mad if you believe a mated shifter could be seduced after being forcibly abducted." Mathis was debating between gutting her with his claws or holding her hostage until he could escape. He had zero interest in fucking her.

"Your tie with Samantha Sinclair has been severed," she murmured as she reached for the other knot.

Shock filled him. "That's not possible."

"Oh, believe me, it is. Shifter mating bonds are trickier than pack bonds or familiar bonds, but we have the means."

Mathis shook his head. His cougar had chosen Sam

above all others. Just knowing she existed somewhere outside of this place made him frantic to reach her, to need her to hold her and breathe in her warm vanilla scent....

His nose twitched as Sam's scent filled the space. Coming from the crazy redhead....

No. Not possible.

The woman smiled that unnerving smile again and victory shone in her eerie eyes. "You see, we know about your kind. Have studied many like you for years. And we know that scent matters to mated males. It's why you can never be unfaithful with another female. The scent is what puts you off. So naturally, I mystically changed mine to match your former mate."

"No." Mathis shook his head which was fogging with her scent. His witch, his Sam. "It doesn't matter whether you smell like her. It changes nothing."

The garment fell away, and she paused by the side of the water bed and looked over her shoulder at him. "You might as well accept the inevitable."

He lunged for her with his claws bared.

Water spurted up between them, preventing his strike. He hissed as his hand breached steaming water, scalding his flesh. With a yell, he retreated until his back hit the outer edge of the bubble.

When the geyser receded, she lay on her side, her arm propped under her head. "The bubble provides you with more than just air. It can sense your intentions. If you move to hurt me in any way, it'll respond to protect me."

His hand trembled and he shut his eyes to block out the pain.

She sighed and then moved toward him, Sam's warm vanilla scent approaching, soothing him. His eyes flashed open. He wouldn't allow her to trick his instincts.

She made a tsking sound. "It'll all go so much easier if you accept me, Mathis. If you breed me."

"Breed you?" He shook his head. "That's what you want? A half-shifter, half whatever the fuck you are, baby? Lady, there are hundreds of us all over the world. Why me?" he snarled. "Why in the hell would you want me?"

She reached for him as though intending to soothe the wound her damn prison had inflicted on him. "It was either you or Damien. Damien Moss is a business owner, as well as former alpha. He would have been missed."

Her implication hurt almost as badly as the burn. The words unspoken but still he heard them clear as day. *No one will miss you.*

Her finger drew down his bare torso. "Deep down you know you come between them, you're in their way. They've been mated for decades, have a son and a grandchild together. A history. What do you provide them with? Sex and scandal. Face facts, to them you are nothing more than a pleasant distraction."

He barely stifled his flinch as her barbs hit home. Hadn't he thought the same thing? But then Damien had said....

What wouldn't Damien say or do to make sure Sam was appeased? An insidious voice whispered. Whenever Sam was overworked or in danger Damien found a way to turn it around on him, to make it his fault.

The redhead moved closer, her manner seductive. "What I'm offering you is a real life. A chance to be a father and a true mate, not a third wheel. Your existence here will serve a purpose. You will help people who badly need it. Your exit from the world above was seamless, your ties severed. There is no other choice for you, Mathis Dracos. Accept me as your mate."

He shook his head, stepped away from her. "Never."

Her soft expression hardened. "Your old life is over. You will remain here until you agree to serve the Collective of Sirenae."

She turned and pressed her hand to the far edge of the bubble. The water parted for her even as the light winked out once more.

Mathis sank to the ground, holding his scalded hand. How the hell would he get out of this?

Her words penetrated the haze of pain and confusion. Collective of Sirenae. That woman was a siren? One of the mythical creatures who could sing and enchant beings to court their own death?

His body trembled and doubt assailed him. If they could make sailors drown themselves at sea or crash their ships upon the rocks, what could they do to him?

Sam

Blinky shuddered as we traveled through the mystical whirlpool.

"There's some sort of drag on the hull," Eric said. "Maybe trusting that creature wasn't the best call."

"Ya think?" Ginny snapped as she held on to her chair. "The pressure gauge is redlining. Or Greenlining. Whatever, it's not good."

"Come on, Blinky," I said to our conveyance. "Keep it together a little longer."

The shuddering grew more intense for a moment and I shut my eyes, not wanting to see the hull breech, or water rushing in to drown us.

Then abruptly the shuddering stopped and Blinky shot forward like it had been fired out of a cannon. I released the joystick and took in the view out the window.

"It's a city," Ginny breathed as she leaned in next to me. "An underwater city."

Indeed that's exactly what it looked like. No cars or vehicles that I could recognize. Instead, beings seemed to float by encased in bubbles through rivers that wound between buildings. Some of them were pulled by tiger sharks or giant rays. And there were structures made from coral that twisted up high spiraling to the dome up above where a giant amber-colored jewel illuminated the streets below.

And the people. I shook my head as I saw them swimming within the current that flowed

around the city like a watery superhighway. They

didn't just travel in bubbles, they wore them, tethered together like colorless pearls. We'd found some of the underwater beings the Goblin Queen had told us about. The question was were they the right beings?

"Where's the trail?" I asked.

"It's gone," Ginny said.

I pushed the joystick to the left and Blinky spun around 180 degrees. Sure enough, the mystical white trail we'd been following was gone.

"Did the spell run out of juice?" I asked.

"It shouldn't have," Ginny said.

We tried casting it again but no trail appeared.

"Now what?" Eric asked.

"We need to talk to someone in there. Question them about the elementals." We sat just outside of the city. To our left, I could see aquatic ferns moving in time with the current but the land beyond the edge of the bubble was bone dry.

"Is there any way we can get through the dome?" Eric asked.

I studied the bubble but other than the part at the top where that amber jewel was located, the structure was one smooth transparent piece.

And then Blinky lurched again. Ginny would have gone flying if Eric hadn't caught her. I slid across the floor as a feeling of weightlessness came over the vehicle.

"What's going on?" I asked as I crawled to the dashboard. I shoved the joystick to the left. The sound of the treads whirred but nothing happened. I shoved it to the right. Same result.

"Pressure's dropping," Eric said. "I think we're caught in one of those bubbles!"

He was right. Blinky had been lifted off the sandy sea floor and drifted on toward the dome. Ginny and I exchanged a panicked look. There was no way to steer. Would we bounce off the dome and back through the whirlpool? Could Blinky handle another trip through that violent gateway?

The second the outer edge of our bubble touched the dome, it seemed to suck us through. My lips parted as we bobbed along the highest waterway. I could see several beings pointing up at us. Two legs, no claws, feathers, or anything that marked them as other. They looked like normal folks from our vantage. Except they all wore garments fashioned out of what looked like thousands and thousands of tiny bubbles.

"Where is this thing taking us?" Eric asked.

Good question. The bubble encasing Blinky had fallen into the current of water that circled the top of the dome. How it stayed suspended above the city was beyond me. Several other bubbles fell in beside us. Some held a single being or a fistful. All were armed with what looked like spears or tridents. None of them looked any friendlier than the tiger sharks who pulled their bubbles like watery chariots.

"Any ideas, Sam?" Ginny asked.

I shook my head. Whatever the beings in this underwater city were, they had us completely at their mercy.

The current swirled around one of the coral spires before releasing us. We drifted down, out of the water accompanied by our cranky-looking guards.

Leaning heavily on my walking stick, I headed back to my seat, trying to ignore the uneasy feeling in my chest.

Ginny gripped Eric's hand. Who knew what awaited us on the other side of Blinky's hull. Would we be able to breathe here? Just because those other creatures could, it didn't mean their bubble atmosphere had the right mix of oxygen for us.

Blinky touched down with a jarring thud. A few moments later a firm pounding on the outer hull echoed through the silent space.

"I think they want in," Eric muttered.

"Can we risk it?" I asked Ginny. "What if we can't breathe?"

"Do you think they'll just let us turn around and leave?" She asked in return.

No, I didn't. Besides, I'd come here for a reason. Sending an entreaty to the universe that I wasn't going to get us all killed, I moved to Blinky's side. "Let us out, pal," I said and put my hand on the bulkhead.

Blinky chirped and then came the whirring sound. No water rushed in, and no poisonous gasses made us suffocate. The air was heavy, but no worse than a humid summer day. Behind me, I heard clothing rustling. Ginny came up to hold my other arm. "Eric's changing. He can defend us better if he's in cougar form."

I covered her hand with my own and squeezed lightly as Blinky lowered the ramp.

The beings holding the spears and tridents rushed inside pointing their weapons at Ginny and Eric.

"Unhand the princess!" One ordered Ginny.

"Princess?" I asked but the question was lost beneath Eric's roar.

The guards yelled, "Shifter!" And then there was a mad scramble as Eric chased them back down the ramp. He stood between them and us, his weight on his front paws, teeth bared in menace.

"Enough!" A voice hollered from behind the swarming guards. "That's enough. Let them pass."

"My liege"— One began but was abruptly cut off.

And then a familiar figure stepped forward. The older man I'd met at the B&B soiree. The one with the snowy white hair and blue eyes. "Caspian?"

He held out his hand to me. "Welcome home, daughter."

CHAPTER 18
SAM

"Daughter?" I stared at him, unable to comprehend.

Caspian's lips curved up, his intense blue eyes filled with conflicting emotion. "Forgive the deception in front of the demon. He is a being that can be useful at times but is not to be trusted."

"Tell me something I don't know," I grumbled.

Heedless of the snarling cougar, Caspian ascended the ramp until he stood a few feet from me. His glance went from me to Eric and back. "Is this one of your mates?"

"Uh....no." He knew I had more than one mate? And that they were cougar shifters? How?

"He's with me," Ginny stepped forward. "Eric, back off. They aren't going to hurt us."

I wouldn't take that one to the bank, Gin. Several of the crabby-looking guards clutched their spears in white-knuckled grips. But Eric did move, allowing Caspian to come closer.

He took my hands in his. "I was hoping you would come home before it was too late."

"Too late?" His hands were warm and smooth, his nails neat and clean. Not a single rough patch or callous. "Too late for what?"

He released his grip on me and waved the comment away. "Let's not talk about unpleasantness. Come, there's so much to show you. We'll have a feast tonight in your honor!" The last boomed out across the square where our bubble had landed.

A cheer went up from the gathered crowd. This was surreal. My brain was scrambled and I couldn't tell if he was insane or maybe I'd hit my head and was hallucinating the whole scene.

"Um, Caspian?" I asked.

"Call me Cas. Or father."

Yeah, that wouldn't be happening. "Cas, then. We wanted to ask about—"

Before I could get the question out another bubble formed over the top of me, Ginny, and Eric. Caspian was encased in another and his royal entourage in a third. We bobbed along behind him pulled by an unknown force.

"Could this be true, Sam?" Ginny was staring at me with wide eyes.

My tongue felt as though it had been glued to the roof of my mouth. "I guess it's possible. I never knew anything about my father. And he looks about the right age."

Eric bared his teeth.

"Yeah, I don't trust it either." I took a deep breath—the air in the bubbles was much cooler and fresher than it had been outside of it. "But for now, we'll just have to keep our eyes and ears open."

Though the reception we received was better than I could have anticipated, I still didn't trust these people. Someone had sent that elemental to terrorize me. To kill Mathis. When I'd set off on my quest to find the elemental that had murdered Mathis never would I have imagined this.

"What are they?" Ginny asked.

I started because I didn't even think to ask. "I don't know. I was thinking we'd run into merpeople or something. But these beings...."

"Look like us." Ginny reached out and squeezed my hand. "Are you holding up okay?"

She was asking about my MS. I did a quick inventory and then frowned. "I feel really...good actually." Fatigue and brain fog were conspicuously absent. No numbness at all. At first, I thought it was because I was so focused on finding the elemental but when was the last time I'd felt so healthy?

Years.

Was it something about this place? Like whatever allowed the streams and rivers to defy the laws of nature also gave me a reprieve from my symptoms?

The bubble floated inside one of the coral buildings and ascended the stairs. Caspian's bubble bobbed in place and then burst, leaving him standing on a raised dais. He stood tall and proud and gestured with his hand, beckoning the bubble closer.

It popped, leaving the three of us standing beside him.

"How do you do that?" I asked him.

He held a ring aloft. Inside was a transparent stone that upon closer inspection looked as though it was filled with colorless soda or carbonated water. "One is issued to every member of our society upon their coming-of-age ceremony. Much more efficient than walking or swimming everywhere. I'll see you are issued one. And your friends of course."

Then he turned to the room and held his hands wide. On the opposite end of the dais a screen appeared, casting an image of my startled face twenty feet into the air. In that booming announcing voice Caspian called, "Collective of Sirenae, I give you, my sole heir and your future queen, Siren Samantha Sinclair!" His words echoed through the city, reverberated off the dome. Somehow he was broadcasting my image to all and sundry in the city.

A roar from outside.

Siren? Future queen? What the actual fuck....?

Before I could argue, the image faded back into a blank wall. Another bubble gulped us up.

"Your rooms are ready for you," Caspian said. "You'll want to freshen up before the banquet."

Was he deliberately trying to put us off for some reason? I didn't get the chance to ask before the bubble floated out of the room and up the stairs. Down a hall and into two bedroom suites connected by a common living room. The décor was the same coral and bubble construction that we were seeing everywhere else in this place.

Once the latest bubble popped, Eric stalked through

the space, probably sniffing for any sign of danger. He returned and shifted. With his lips curving up he performed an elegant bow. "All clear, your highness."

I rolled my eyes, even as my heart lurched. He reminded me so much of Mathis that a pang went through me.

"So," Ginny said as she tossed Eric his clothes. "Do you trust him?"

"My supposed father?" I shrugged and then moved to the window, which was a series of bubble layers. "He was at the B&B the night Mathis was attacked. That was the first time I ever saw him and the timing is...suspicious."

"Agreed," Eric muttered. "Royal fathers don't come out of freaking nowhere and proclaim you the future monarch without having a hidden agenda."

When Ginny and I both stared at him he shrugged. "What? I watch movies."

"As ridiculous as he can be, my husband is right," Ginny said. "Something smells fishy, and I don't mean literally. Why is this the first you've heard from Caspian? And did you catch what he said about before it's too late? Even if he doesn't have anything to do with what happened to Mathis, there are things he's not telling you."

I nodded and then looked out the window, took in the sight of people bobbing along in their bubbles. "Sirens," I whispered.

"Makes sense considering your singing voice," Eric murmured.

I swallowed. I wished I could talk to my mates about

this. But one was gone and the other one completely out of reach.

We were on our own.

I PERFORMED a sponge bath with an actual sea sponge while remaining in my gray dress. If the sirens didn't like it, tough shit. I still wasn't ready to wear anything else. Someone knocked on the door to my bedroom. Figuring it was Ginny coming to check on me, I gripped the coral handle and yanked the heavy door inward.

The other man I'd met at the B&B stood on the other side. Instead of his dark suit, he wore the same sort of toga bubble fabric that everyone else in this place sported.

"Oh, uh, hi. Wade, right?"

"That's correct, my intended." Without invitation, he crossed the threshold to my room.

"Your intended?" I scowled at him. "What are you talking about?"

"That's right." He moved toward me in a way that I really didn't like. "You were promised to me at birth, the second you set foot in Atlantis."

Atlantis? That's what this place was? Add it to the growing pile of info that was bending my mind. I needed to nip this intended thing in the bud, pronto.

"Whoa there, buddy." I put my hands up. "I don't even *know* you. And I never agreed to become the queen.

Plus, I'm in a relationship already so...." I gestured to the door clearly indicating he should fuck directly off. Too bad I didn't have any more of that banishing oil.

Wade moved closer and my stomach twisted. *Wrong.* He wasn't either of my guys and if he tried anything I'd use my walking stick to nail him in the crotch.

"Of course, you'll become queen." He said it as though I were a difficult child. At least he'd stopped moving closer.

"Says who?" I lifted my chin.

"It is your destiny. Our destiny to rule this place and oversee the return to glory for the Collective."

"Look, Wade. I'm sure you're a nice guy," I lied. From what I'd seen and heard he was a smarmy social climbing turd who had gone power mad. "But I'm not staying here." I gestured again to the door.

His eyes narrowed and he glared down at me but before he could speak, someone else knocked on the still open door.

"Come in," I said in a rush.

Caspian strode forward and frowned when he spotted the other man. "Am I interrupting?"

I shook my head even as Wade dipped his head in a slight bow. "I was just leaving."

I sagged against the coral wall as he strode out the door.

"Are you well, Samantha? You look pale." Caspian asked. "Come, sit." He gestured to a coral chair that didn't look even slightly comfortable.

"I'm fine," I said. "Though I think I pissed Wade off by not agreeing to co-rule with him."

Caspian's white brows drew together. "Wade has been awaiting your return his whole life. Even after we discovered that you were mated to shifters. He's stubborn but deep down, he only wants what is best for the Collective."

"And what's best in his mind is hooking up with me, the future queen who a day ago didn't even know this side of her lineage?" My voice grew shrill.

Caspian sighed and took a seat in the coral chair. "I know this is a lot for you to process Samantha."

"Sam," I corrected. "Only bill collectors and telemarketers call me Samantha."

Lines appeared around his eyes and mouth as he smiled. "Sam, then. Ask me anything and I'll do my level best to give you an honest answer."

I thought it through and even though questions sped through my mind, there was only one thing that I needed to know. "Did you order the elemental to stalk and terrorize us so I would come here?"

The expression of shock on his face was so genuine that I knew the answer before he spoke. "What?"

I sagged down onto the bubble bed. "An elemental has been harassing me." That was as much as I wanted to reveal to this man who said he was my father.

Caspian was shaking his head slowly, his snowy hair moving like seaweed. "They're our guardians, protectors of the portal between this place and your world."

So that thing we'd seen on the Monitor was one of them as well. "It's been leaving me notes signed *your secret admirer*. We cast an echoes spell and saw it drag something into the water." My throat closed up.

Caspian leaned forward and gripped my hand. "Samantha, I swear to you on your mother's grave that I did not authorize an elemental to harass you. Even to save your life, I wouldn't do such as you're describing."

"What do you mean to save my life?" I searched his blue eyes. "What aren't you telling me?"

"You're sick, are you not?" He gestured to my walking stick. "A chronic disease that has plagued you for several years?" At my nod, he continued. "And how have you felt since you came here?"

"Pretty good, physically," I wondered what he was getting at.

Caspian sighed. "It's because of your mixed heritage. Half of you is a white witch, an energy worker, and a Healer. The other half is Siren, a powerful product of my line, just as your brother was."

"Ray?" I whispered. "This...condition killed my brother? Why in the hell didn't you come to us? To tell him?"

"For the same reason, I couldn't tell you. There's a geas on all those who live in Atlantis. We can not reveal our species to any who do not find their way here on their own. It keeps us safe."

"So you chose to let my brother die? To let me die? Talk about a deadbeat dad." Why did that hurt so much? I'd lived my entire life knowing nothing about him. How could he have the power to wound me this way?

"A geas isn't a choice, it's a mystical compulsion. And it has benefited us. I yearned to go to you and your brother, Sam. But I'd already broken the rules when I brought your mother here. She was a witch and she bound herself to our rules as well just so she could be with me for a few precious months." His smile turned fond. "You don't remember me at all?"

When I shook my head, his smile turned sad. "When you were about four, I longed to see you. Your mother took you to an island and we met in secret. I watched you play for hours, singing to yourself all the while. You have the most beautiful voice."

Out of the murky depths of my Swiss cheese brain, the image surfaced. A warm beach. Sitting in a hammock with this man, singing my favorite song at the time, *Big Rock Candy Mountain*.

The breath escaped me even as he continued, "If it were possible, I would have stayed there forever, our little paradise by the sea. It was where we conceived Ray." His eyes glinted. "She was the love of my life."

That made no sense to me. "Then why weren't you together?"

"A bird may love a fish but where would they make a home? My place was here. And she tried to stay with me but being cut off from her coven felt as unnatural to her as being on land was to me."

I shook my head. Too many emotions churned through me. Leading the pack was that mistress of destruction, Wrath. I felt as if she would burst free of my chest at any moment, emerging from me in a cloud of a thousand bats and swoop through Atlantis.

"Tell me more about this illness," I said through clenched teeth. "Do people have it here?"

He shook his head. "The symptoms are widespread, and mortals have different names for them but in the end, the result is always the same. Debilitation and eventually death."

"What are you saying?" I breathed the question, already fearing the answer.

"That if you stay here, with us, you'll be well again." His blue eyes locked on me. "But if you return to the land above, you'll sicken more and more… until you die."

CHAPTER 19
SAM

True to his word, Caspian had the rings to control the bubbles made for each of us. Ginny and Eric decided to go out exploring. After all, how often did anyone get a chance to sightsee in the city of Atlantis? I stayed in my room, sprawled in my silver dress on my bubble bed.

Water will be your salvation. Water will be your doom. You need to know the truth about your father, Sam. You must know what you are. My mother had told me that. What she hadn't said was that she was a witch and my father a siren. I wasn't just a halfway decent singer the way I always thought. It was part of my mystical heritage.

Shouldn't a woman in her fifties know what she was? Bad enough Damien and Alba had kept the truth from me for "my own good." But then to find out my parents had done the same fucking thing...

Wrath slithered around inside me, looking for an outlet. It would be so easy to unleash her on Caspian, and this place. After all, one of their supposed guardians had drowned Mathis.

Mathis...I wonder what he would think of the current shitshow. I shut my eyes but not before a tear streaked down my cheek. I could almost hear his voice.

Doesn't change a thing, little witch. You are who you are, and I love every bit of it.

What if I go dark? I whispered to the shifter who was nothing more than a memory. It was a real worry. I wanted to give myself over to dark spells. I wanted to summon demons to seek vengeance on the elemental that had ripped my heart in half and dragged it into the sea. Part of me wanted to learn Necromancy. To retrieve Mathis from the grave. It was the darkest of all magics and there was no coming back to being a Healer after that. I wouldn't stop there either. I'd get my brother, and then I'd resurrect my dead mother so I could ask her why she had never told me or Ray that she was a witch who loved a siren. Or what fate had in store for us. Or for her.

I frowned. That wasting sickness that Caspian spoke of...why had it killed my mother, who was by all accounts, a witch? She should have been immune.

Too many unanswered questions. But in the end, did they even matter?

Restless, I got up and grabbed my walking stick, though I barely needed it for balance and then stalked to the window and looked down at Atlantis. Sirens. Hidden and protected in their enchanted city. What cause would any of them have to want me here? Caspian seemed fit in mind and body even if his parental skills were questionable.

Just then a bubble broke from the stream. I stepped back as Ginny and Eric appeared in the window.

"That is so fun," Ginny exclaimed when their bubble burst. "You've got to try it, Sam."

"Maybe later. How's Blinky doing?"

"Well, enough. There are more bio mechanoids like him in the royal stables. That's what the stablemaster told me they call sentient beasts that are part machine and part living creatures. They're bringing him a change of fluids as well as doing a full diagnostic for the princess's conveyance."

I made a disgusted sound and turned away.

"Sam," Ginny put her hand on my shoulder. "I know this must be upsetting for you. But we're here if you need anything from us."

I swallowed past the lump in my throat. "The mission hasn't changed. We need to find out who my secret admirer is and how they're controlling the elemental that killed Mathis. I already asked Caspian and I think he was truthful that he knew nothing about it. Then again, he's in the habit of keeping secrets."

"Then we need a truth serum," Ginny moved to where she'd left her backpack and began to dig for ingredients. "I'll brew up a triple batch. It'll be enough for us to question three people. The banquet tonight is the perfect excuse. Slip it into the drink of whoever you want to speak truth to you and they'll spill their guts—so to speak."

"And how do we keep them from raising the alarm about why we're really here after we're done interrogating them?" I asked.

"We can kill them," Eric suggested.

When Ginny glared at him he shrugged. "What? It's a way of keeping someone quiet for good."

"Those elementals protect this place and the people here," I said to him. "You saw what one of them can do. It's unstoppable. Imagine if we have a host of them bearing down on our community. Better to not start a war to find one psycho."

Ginny was busy picking through random crystals. "I think perhaps the best thing we can do is mick them with a forgetfulness powder. It's like being intoxicated. The being will wake up hungover with fuzzy memories. I don't have everything I need for that here though. We'll have to find some seaberries. I spotted a garden when we were flying over the city."

"I remember. I'll go harvest them," Eric offered.

"I'll go with you." It was better than hanging out in this room, brooding. Besides, I didn't want Wrath's throbbing energy to influence Ginny's potion.

Eric stepped up on the windowsill and I joined him. "Hold out your ring," he said.

When I did as instructed, he added, "Now, picture the bubble forming around us. Keeping us safe, making us weightless."

I did and nothing happened. I frowned at my ring. "Maybe mine is broken?"

"Do you really think the king would give his long-lost daughter a defective ring?" Eric cocked a brow.

When I shook my head he added, "It takes some real visualizing, at least that's what Ginny said. There can't be any of this fence-sitting *what if this doesn't work* naysayer crap in your mind."

I was thinking exactly that and flushed when Eric called me out. Everyone else here was doing it, so I had to be able to do it too. Easy breezy bubble squeezy.

"Close your eyes and try again and this time believe it with your whole body. Feel it."

Shutting my eyes, I felt it. Deriving memories from the last few times we'd been encased in bubbles. How the air was cleaner, less humid than the whole of Atlantis. Then I took a deep breath and imagined Eric and I floating above the town.

And when my lids lifted...we were. "Holy shit."

"I know, right?" Eric grinned from ear to ear.

We bobbed along, looking down at the city and its inhabitants. It could have been New York or L.A. below us. Any city in the world. The way the sirens just went about their business, stopping to chat with one another. They varied in height, skin tone, mannerisms. Some were thin, others like me had a good amount of junk in the trunk. I'd never seen so many supernatural beings in one place. They looked so...normal.

Eric's palms pressed against the bubble. "Amazing, isn't it?"

I swallowed. "How are you doing it?"

He glanced over at me. "Doing what?"

I turned to look down at the crowd. We were drifting over a park where itty bitty sirens climbed over gym equipment. "Keeping your spirits up. I want to sink into this pit of despair and let it consume me."

Eric's expression sobered. "Sam, I know. And I get it. I

miss him like a limb. But you must go on because other people need you to. It's what he would want for you. For all of us."

Tears stung my eyes and I turned to look out at the city. "I wish he could have seen this place."

"He'd be happy for you." Eric hesitated. "And if you decide you need to stay, we get it."

"Stay?" I blinked at him. "You heard my discussion with Caspian?"

"Shifter hearing." He shrugged. "But if you need to stay for your health, Damien will understand."

Damien always understood. And I would never ask him to come here either. He had a restaurant and a community and a son and a granddaughter. A life.

"I'm not gonna lie, Eric. It's tempting. I haven't felt this good in years." I was holding the walking stick for the same reason I wore the silver dress. Both reminded me of Mathis.

"I hear a but in there," Eric said.

"But, I don't trust these people. Someone here has been using an elemental to terrorize us. Maybe more than one person. How could I ever trust people that would hide Mathis's killer from us?"

Eric put a hand on my shoulder and squeezed. "The gardens Ginny spied are over there."

I visualized the bubble drifting out of the current and toward the gardens. They were at the outer edge of the dome from where we'd first entered. That was when I spotted it. "Look."

"What am I looking at?" Eric scanned the shadowy

area beyond the garden wall where an elemental skulked.

The watery being glowed with a white aura, just like the one we'd followed from the world above.

Wrath opened one eye and whispered a single word. *Now.*

"Sam," Eric still held my shoulder and he shook it, almost violently. "Sam, you can't. Those things are invincible. We don't even know if it can be killed."

"No," I agreed. "But we can sure as hell follow it."

Mathis rolled over and looked up into the face of the female who'd stolen Sam's scent.

"Would you like me to heal your hand?" she asked.

"No." As much as the healing burns hurt, he would rather have the pain keep him alert. Remind him what these people were willing to do.

She sighed. "Mathis Dracos, I'm not the villain here. No matter what you think, I saved your life."

He didn't ask her what she was talking about because he felt sure that was exactly what she wanted.

"Our people are dying," she breathed. "Our human halflings are weak, like your Samantha."

"Sam's a siren?" He scowled. "How is that possible?"

"She's the daughter of our king. Surely, you've seen how she suffered on land. How the mortal physicians can do nothing for her."

He didn't know if he believed anything his captor told him, but he'd hear her out. "Sam's not weak."

"Her body betrays her on land. She's stronger than the others. Her brother didn't even make it to thirty. But she bore a son."

"John," he nodded.

"A healthy son with a shifter." Tears glinted in her eyes. "So many of our babes are malformed. They don't live for a full day. And those that do must stay here. The halflings are stronger, but living on land hurts them as well. You have no idea what a miracle John Moss is. Healthy, strong. Shifters will be our salvation."

Despite his situation, Mathis felt a small stirring of pity for her. "How many children did you lose?"

"Seventeen," she whispered.

"I'm sorry." He was.

She dashed away her tears. "Yet you still stubbornly refuse to help me?"

"Even if I wasn't mated to Sam, if she wasn't in my heart and soul, I don't want kids." It was the first time he'd ever said the words out loud. "I don't want to pass on my family's crazy. Shifters have been known to eat their young to retain power. This world is too violent, too fucked up. I wouldn't inflict that on an innocent."

She stared at him for a long minute. "If you agree to help me, to help us, I'll return you to Sam."

"You'll let me go back to land?"

She shook her head. "I don't need to. The princess has returned to us." Even as Mathis's heart leapt he noted that the siren didn't seem happy about that.

"You're sure it's Sam?" Had she come after him? How?

"She is here, as is your twin. If you agree to help us, I'll release you to stay with her." Her lips twisted as though the offer tasted bitter.

"Sam won't stay here," he shook his head. "Even if she is your...princess."

"Only in Atlantis can she be well. All those of siren blood are healed by the sea."

Mathis stared at her for a long moment, trying to assess if she was lying. But unlike Sam's scent, hers didn't change with her mood or emotions.

Bed this siren and live with his mate in this place? Was that to be his compromise? No, he would agree to nothing until he could talk to Sam. "What's your name?"

"Willa," she looked at him with hopeful eyes.

"Willa." He nodded. "Let me see Sam. Let me talk to her."

"No," she shook her head violently. "No, he would be furious."

"He who?"

But she was already heading to the edge of the bubble.

"Wait!" Mathis reached for her but she'd already crossed the boundary of his bubble, leaving him once again in the dark.

CHAPTER 20

SAM

"Where have you two been?" Ginny asked as she paced the common area of our adjoining suites. "Guards keep knocking to ask if Princess Samantha is ready to go down to her banquet and I have to keep putting them off."

"Sorry, Gin." Eric moved to her side and brushed a soft kiss on her cheek before handing her the berries we'd collected.

Her eyes went wide. "Sorry? That's all I get—"

"It was my fault," I said. "We spotted the elemental with the white aura trail. It crossed the dome bubble though and I insisted we wait to see if it came back. Long story short, it didn't."

Ginny nodded and then cast me a look of sympathy. "I think I have just enough time to get our dust done before someone shows back up." She handed a vial with a cloudy but colorless liquid to each of us. "Add that to any beverage and it will meld and become undetectable by whomever it is you want to question."

Eric and I had talked about it when we were waiting by the dome for any sign of the murderous elemental. I would interrogate Caspian and Ginny would take Wade, who struck me as the sort of guy to underestimate a female, even if she was a powerful witch. Eric had decided to interrogate one of the servers who often saw and heard more than the people they worked for even realized.

Eric pocketed his serum and then sprinted to the wardrobe where the bubble clothing that had been left for him was laid out.

"You're not changing?" Ginny asked.

"Not for anyone," I muttered. The silver dress was stained, torn in places, and looked nowhere near as alluring as it had when I'd first put it on. It had become my talisman. I would remove it for good only after I discovered the identity of my secret admirer.

She squeezed the berry juice on top of a salt-like component. It didn't behave the way I would have expected, making the dry ingredients clump together. Instead, it seemed to break them up into an even finer powder so light that some of it floated in the air like dust motes.

"Did you have any trouble finding this?" Ginny asked.

I shook my head. "All I had to do was ask and a very helpful siren put down the basket she was using and made a beeline for the plant."

"Must be good to be the long-lost princess." She poured the powder into small pouches and then handed it to me. Not having a purse and not wanting to carry my backpack to the banquet, I stuffed it and the tiny vile in my bra.

Ginny clucked and picked up her hairbrush. "The dress I get, Sam, but you should make a little bit of an effort to look like royalty."

I let her brush out my hair, missing Damien's claws. "Hey, Gin?"

"Yeah?"

"Be careful with Wade. He's suspect number one in my book."

"Then why aren't you questioning him?"

Because I need to know firsthand if Caspian has been lying to me. He was the king and would have the power to command an elemental. Would he have killed my mate just so I would come here...to save me from my sickness? To be his royal successor?

Means. Motive, Opportunity. I couldn't rule him out, no matter how much I wanted to.

My hands clenched into fists as she pinned my hair on top of my head. There was more I wanted to say to her. Hell, I wanted to tell her to take Eric right to Blinky and make for the dome as fast as they could. Because if Wrath caught sight of that elemental again, she wanted to blow this place to Kingdom Come.

I needed answers. Wrath needed vengeance.

I tried to think about all those blameless people we'd seen milling through Atlantis. Wrath sneered, *casualties are inevitable in war. The sirens started it. We will end it.*

Much like my body connection, she was growing stronger here. Was Wrath really my siren half? I'd begun to suspect that was the case. She was so cold, so bloodthirsty.

So powerful.

Ginny and Eric would fight me if they knew what I struggled with. Wasn't that why they insisted on coming with me in the first place? So I let her fuss with my hair until Eric emerged at the same time as someone knocked on the outer door.

"Come in," I called.

Caspian swung the door inward, and his blue eyes met mine. "Is everything all right? The guards said you weren't feeling well...?"

"I'm fine," I lied. Pasting on a smile, I created a new bubble to carry us down to the banquet.

Having to slip someone a truth serum roofie was more difficult than I would have imagined. Not that I'd spent a ton of time imagining it. But as the newly arrived princess, it seemed there was always someone watching me, studying me, judging my stained silver dress that was not made of bubbles like everyone else's. I spotted Wade the minute we entered the great gathering space and his eyes narrowed in obvious disapproval.

Eat a dick, intended.

I caught Ginny's gaze and jerked my chin toward him. She looped her arm through Eric's and on cue said, "We're gonna go mingle."

"See you on the flip side," I muttered.

Caspian wasted no time introducing me to the sirens of his court. All were surprised to meet me. I gathered it wasn't often that the Siren halflings found their way to Atlantis. Probably because no one freaking told them what they were. Wrath seethed like an eel inside me. These people were pampered, healthy, and had time to attend a fancy state banquet while Ray was dead. Mathis was dead.

I tuned out after a few minutes. Names and faces blurred together. Pasting a phony smile on my face, I resorted to the sort of pleasantries that humans make even though they don't usually mean them. "So nice to meet you. Love your bubble design, that's the first I've seen with a waistcoat."

Apparently the bubble garments were part of the ring's magic, the limitation of the design was the wearer's imagination.

The hardest were the questions, especially about my mother. "I remember her well. Arresting witch and quiet a temper." One plump siren male with a body like a barrel chuckled. He wore toga-esque bubbles around his burly frame. "Didn't she try to take the curse off of you? I seem to recall her spending hours in the library looking for a way to transfer the siren's curse from her offspring to herself." His gaze went to my walking stick before darting away. "I guess it didn't entirely work."

My pulse pounded. Was that why she'd been sick with the bizarre wasting disease called the siren's curse even though she hadn't been a siren or even a halfling? Wouldn't I do the same for John or Emily?

My heart almost stopped as a thought surfaced. I turned to face Caspian. "Will John or my granddaughter have to deal with the curse too?"

"No." It was a female who answered me, one with flame-red hair and eyes so pale there was hardly any distinguishing between the whites and her irises. "Your son is immune to the curse as are any of his offspring."

I sagged in relief even as Wrath whispered, *"Good, let's end the rest of them."*

Tamping my inner bloodlust down, I strove to pay attention as Caspian made the introductions with the dead-eyed redheaded siren. "Samantha, this is Dr. Willa Graves, the head of our biomedical research team."

"I've been studying your medical records since you were born," Willa said.

"And exactly how did you get ahold of them?" I grated.

Caspian looked uncomfortable. "Well, when you were younger your mother sent them to us."

"And after?" I raised a brow.

"We sent the elementals to retrieve them of course," Willa said. Either she was tone-deaf or a total bitch. "It's a matter of our survival after all."

I was prepared to rail against her for daring to invade my privacy that way but she'd said something far more intriguing. "You control the elementals? How?"

"Our rings," Caspian interjected. "Before my time only the ruling family could command

the elementals but we've found it necessary to invite a few key persons in leadership roles to dispatch the guardians as needed."

My heart pounded as I asked, "And how many people have access to the elementals?"

Willa shrugged. "At least a hundred. Since I have you here I was hoping to get a blood sample from you. Run a few tests with our technology, maybe answer a few of the questions that have been plaguing me."

I forced a smile so brittle I wouldn't have been surprised if my whole face cracked. A hundred people could command those beings. Including two standing in front of me.

"Let's let the princess settle in for a few more days before we poke and prod her." Caspian had better understanding of my mood than the Dr. Of course I'd had more than my fair share of curt bedside manner.

Treat the symptoms, not the patient. I'd dealt with it for years. And when I'd fought them on a test or treatment, they condescended to me.

"It's for your own good, Samantha. Your insurance will cover it, don't worry."

They never understood that it wasn't about the money. It was about the lack of dignity being a patient gave me. The lack of compassion from those who were supposed to care for me. "It won't make me better, though."

"No, but if we understand it better maybe we can treat more people in the future…."

Like that was enough reason to be a fucking guinea pig.

Blinking back to the moment I asked. "Where's the nearest restroom?"

"Right outside the hall. Willa, will you be a dear and show her?"

"Of course, sire." Willa gestured and her bubble dress rippled as she wound through the crowd with me trailing in her wake.

I spied Eric talking to a guy with a serving tray though there was no sign of Ginny or Wade. The vial of truth serum pressed hard against my breasts. Going with an impulse I plucked two glasses of whatever effervescent liquid was being served off a table. I followed Willa into a large room that was more of a lounge and the sort of public bathrooms I was used to. She gestured to a door but I held up my glass. "Just going to finish this first."

She disappeared within. The second the door shut, I dug the vial out and popped the lid. After dumping one glass into a nearby fern, I added the serum to it and then topped it with liquid from the other glass.

When Willa emerged, I handed her the full glass. "A toast. To finding a cure for the curse."

She took the glass and raised it to mine. I sipped, even as my heart pounded and I watched her bring her own glass up to her pouty red lips and take the smallest sip. Ginny had assured me it was undetectable and Willa didn't scream that I was trying to poison her so I figured she was right.

How long would it take the serum to kick in? I polished off my own glass and then went into the bathroom. The toilet was thankfully not coral and looked typical.

"Where does your technology come from?" I asked Willa through the door.

"The guardians steal what we require from the world above."

I frowned as I flushed and then washed my hands at the sink before opening the door.

The slender woman was leaning against the counter, her gaze studying my every move. "The elementals. They protect our realm, keep us safe here. Get whatever we need. Though they can't make what we need do our bidding."

She frowned as though she hadn't meant to say that last part out loud.

I decided to test the waters, so to speak. "Hey Willa, what do you really think of me?"

Her answer was prompt with no time or effort devoted to politeness or politic. "You're a spoiled and selfish woman who spent much of her life feeling sorry for herself even though she'd been given the greatest gift —a healthy child."

Her hand flew to her mouth but it was too late. The words were already out.

She made for the door to the outside but I was faster. I threw my back against it and brandished my walking stick. "Tell me about the curse."

"No one knows where the curse came from," she answered, even as her gaze darted around looking for another escape. "In the last few generations we've had higher and higher infant mortality rate and even the halflings are frail. All save one"

I frowned. "Only one?"

She nodded. "Your son, John. The child of a witch

siren hybrid and a shifter. The shifters will be our salvation."

My lips parted. "Are you kidding me?"

Sweat began to bead on her forehead and her hands shook. "Please, no more."

"Oh sweetie pie," I crooned. "We are just getting started."

She trembled all over as though I'd personally threatened her. Her pale eyes didn't look so dead when they darted to and fro, hunting for a way out. Why was she so nervous?

I didn't know how long the serum would last and couldn't waste a second. "Do you know who controls the elemental who has been stalking me?"

"Yes." Her body spasmed.

"Who was it?" I snarled. "Who ordered the being to kill Mathis?"

Her words sent me into orbit. "He's not dead."

My heart stopped. "What are you talking about? We saw the thing drag him underwater."

"He told me to do it, to command the elemental to kill him. But I could use him. All that was needed was for you to think he was dead. So, I took him. Ordered the guardian to capture him instead." Her eyes filled with tears. "I reproduced your scent, wore it to fool his mating instinct. I want a child to live, just like you've had! If our child survives we'll know we've found a way to circumvent the curse!"

She was babbling, pleading, snot running down her nose. My brain had shorted out when she said *our child*. No, Mathis wouldn't. He couldn't.

It would break him, being used like that again.

Had she succeeded? I stared down at her flat stomach beneath her empire waist bubble gown. If she had I couldn't kill her.

Yet. Wrath whispered.

He was alive. And I wanted him back.

"Where is he?" I snarled. "Where is Mathis?"

Willa's eyes rounded. "My lab. It's outside the bubble."

If this bitch had hurt Mathis in any way, I would have her guts for garters. Gripping her by the hair I snarled. "You're going to take me to him right fucking now."

CHAPTER
TWENTY-ONE

Every time Damien walked Wally and Wilma they headed toward the ocean. He wondered if the corgis could sense Sam even beneath the waves. He hadn't been able to sense her at all since the door to that goblin vehicle had sealed shut. Not knowing if she was safe made his stomach acid churn.

Wally barked at the sea spray. Damien crouched low and scratched him behind his pointed ears. "I know fella, I miss her too."

"Damien!"

He turned to see Fran and Ivan heading toward him. The Russian was dressed in his customary black slacks and turtleneck that made his countenance even more dour and imposing. Fran wore a white eyelet skirt and peasant blouse that exposed her freckled shoulders. Damien stared down at his dirty jeans and rumpled t-shirt. He hadn't bothered to shower or change since Sam had left.

He raised a hand toward the couple, hoping they

were just being sociable and that they would steer clear of him as everyone else had been doing. No such luck. They headed right for him and the corgis.

"I've been thinking," Fran said. "About Sam's ex-husband, the energy vampire. We all remarked at how strong he was and how it was amazing she was able to deal with him for all that time. You and Mathis both said it only took him a short time to drain you."

Damien nodded. "What has that got to do with anything?"

"The fact that a witch, and no offense but a white witch who didn't even know what she was managed to sustain an energy vampire for years and survive..." Fran brush stray hair out of her eyes. "It's highly unlikely."

"The energy vampire is gone. Yet Sam is no better." Ivan said. "Fran mentioned she appears worse of late."

Damien frowned. He wouldn't betray Sam's trust by confirming that she had been declining but if what they were saying was true..."You think there might be another energy vampire draining her?"

"*Net*" Ivan shook his head. "The rest of us would have felt its effect."

"We think that Sam was actually immune to the energy vampire, at least partly," Fran added. "And whatever it is that gave her that immunity is part of her unknown heritage. Maybe you could talk to John, find out if he knows anything about his grandparents?"

Mental forehead smack. Damien hadn't even considered calling his son. Sam had asked him not to until after she left. And then he didn't want to talk to anyone.

He frowned as something dawned on him. "In the

echo reproduction, we saw Mathis on the phone with someone. It wasn't me or Sam and he had just been patrolling with Eric. We'd asked John to investigate something about Sam's heritage for us. Maybe that's what he was doing."

Whistling for the corgis, Damien pivoted on his heel and sprinted for the trailer. His heart had gone from barely beating to thundering against his ribs. A clue, lying on their bedroom floor all this time and he'd been so distracted he hadn't put it together.

He threw the screen door open with enough force that he ripped out the pressure bar. It sagged cockeyed but he didn't care as he sprinted down the hall.

The bedroom floor was messy, covered with doggie tumbleweeds and sand. He had a Roomba they used only when dogs were outside as Wally and Wilma liked to bark and attack the vacuum. If it had been going at any point since the night Mathis was attacked, it could have pushed the phone under the bed.

Dropping to his belly he slithered under the bedframe, letting his eyes adjust to the dim space. There, up near the headboard, he saw an oblong rectangle. Mathis's phone.

He snatched it up and prayed it had some battery left. No such luck. Mathis's charger was out in the living room. He ran for it just as Fran and Ivan hit the top step. His hands shook as he plugged the phone in.

The dark screen lit up and he immediately tried to swipe it open. It asked for a thumbprint identification. He growled in frustration. Damn Mathis and his cagy ways.

"Allow me." Ivan took the phone and muttered something under his breath. Pressing his own thumb to the screen and more muttering, then he handed it back to Damien, unlocked.

"That's handy," Damien grinned and then swiped the screen open. Accessed the call history.

Sure enough the last one was from John.

He dialed his son's number.

"Dad," John answered on the first ring. "Mathis?"

Tears pricked Damien's eyes. He hadn't realized how badly he wanted to hear his son's voice. "No, it's me."

"Is everything all right?" John asked. "I tried texting mom a few times but no one picked up."

"No. We have a situation here." Damien's throat went dry. He knew Sam had intended to go dark by killing whatever being had sent the elemental to harass them. He knew her mission was a suicide mission. But damn it he hoped that by asking Eric and Ginny to go with her that she would think twice. She would protect her friends, no matter what.

Briefly, he explained all that had happened to John.

"So you're saying she's under the ocean, hunting for whoever took Mathis?"

"Whoever killed Mathis." Damien couldn't believe he hadn't been clear on that point.

"Not necessarily." John didn't sound distraught.

Damien gripped the phone as tightly as he could. "What do you mean?"

"My grandmother, mom's mom I mean, she was taken under the water. Came back pregnant with mom. I told Mathis all this. I guess he didn't catch you up?"

"He didn't have a chance." Damien put out a hand on the doorframe, so he didn't topple over. His head swam with this new information.

"Do you think she'll find her father?" John asked. "That maybe he might help her find her secret admirer?"

Damien's gaze shifted to the churning sea. "Honestly, son. I don't know what the fuck to think anymore."

Sam

My hands shook as I followed Willa out of the bathroom. Mathis was alive. And she was going to take me to him. Or die bloody.

Wrath had wrapped around my heart and lungs and squeezed with all her might. She wanted to kill the siren that dared to try and steal my mate. I agreed, but if she'd succeeded in fooling his instincts, she might be pregnant. I needed to get word to Eric and Ginny though I loathed to go back into that ballroom and face Caspian. If I discovered that he knew about this, there would be no holding Wrath in check.

Pulling on the shifter bonds I hunted for the yellow-gold one that represented Eric and gave it a commanding tug. I couldn't speak to him telepathically the way that Damien and Mathis, Mel and Javier could, but the mental tether would let him know where I was and that I wanted him to come find me.

Within moments he emerged from the ballroom, Ginny by his side. "Sam? I haven't had a chance to—"

"Mathis is alive," I told him and jerked my head to the siren. "She's been holding him captive. She's going to take us to him, right now."

Eric's claws shot out. His lips peeled back from his teeth in a menacing snarl. "Where is he?"

Ginny put a hand on his arm, probably the only thing that was keeping him from full out shifting and tearing the siren's throat out.

"At my laboratory," she quaked with fear, leaning back toward me as if I were the safer option. How wrong she was.

"Samantha?" Wade appeared and offered me his hand. "I was wondering if you'd grace me with a dance?"

I didn't miss the way his gaze slid to Willa and then back to me.

"Is he your accomplice?" I asked the siren. "Is he the one who intended to kill Mathis?"

Her eyes were wide, and she trembled all over as if fighting the compulsion to answer truthfully. "Yes."

Eric lunged for Wade, The man wrapped himself in a bubble and vanished up through the open window.

When it looked as though Eric intended to chase after Wade, I barked out a command. "Stop. We need to find your brother."

All the shifter's muscles were tense, but he nodded slowly and then turned to face Willa. "Take us to him."

He seized her arm and barked, form a bubble. I'd

never seen Eric so on edge. More proof that one didn't have to be an alpha to have a temper.

"What's going on here?" Caspian strode up scanning our faces with a frown. He stopped on mine.

"Tell him," Eric shook Willa's arm. The Siren had begun sobbing prettily, her hand reaching for Caspian.

"She has another," she begged her king. "Another male, and she's had a son. I only wanted to see if it was possible."

"If what were possible?" Caspian glared at her.

"She took Mathis. She wants to breed with him and have a strong offspring, like John."

The king paled, shook his head. His lips parted and for a moment I thought he didn't know what to say.

The sound that emerged from his lips was unlike anything I'd ever heard before.

Eric clapped his hands over his sensitive ears as the walls of the coral palace shook. Willa fell to the ground, her sobs turning into screams. It seemed as if the entire dome quaked under the auditory onslaught.

I lurched forward and put my hands on Caspian's bubble-clad shoulder. "Stop!"

He did though I thought that whatever had caused him to quit had nothing to do with my plea.

A shiver stole over me as I looked up. Elementals had formed around us their blank faces terrifying.

He looked around them all, the beings that provided for his society. "Which of them did it?"

Was this to be some form of justice? I looked around but there was no sign of the elemental with the whitish trail. Either the spell had worn off or it wasn't present. "I don't think that one's here."

Blood dripped from Willa's nose and ears, and she crawled on her hands and knees toward us. "Forgive me, my king. Wade said we needed to act to bring your daughter home. He wanted to kill one of her mates, to drag him beneath the sea. That he knew Samantha would follow and she would be saved from the curse."

He stared down at Willa with blazing blue eyes. Her hand was raised as she pleaded for mercy.

"You will take us to where you've been holding her mate," he ordered. "And then you will tell us everything."

Mathis lay on his side in the dark. It was so silent here. His cougar wanted to run to prowl to follow scents and hear something other than the buzzing of his own thoughts. The thought that Sam was nearby, that he couldn't sense her anymore, broke his heart. He was in an impossible position. If he refused Willa, she would never let him see Sam. And if he accepted her agreement, Sam would never forgive him.

He hoped Damien was keeping her safe. But Willa hadn't mentioned him. She had mentioned Eric. And where Eric went, Ginny would follow. At least she wasn't alone.

Suddenly the light came on, brighter than before. He winced and curled in on himself. He still didn't know what to say. It wasn't in his nature to waffle but Willa would want an answer. Maybe if he could convince her that there was another way, that Sam, with her big generous Healer's heart would help the Collective find it but only if she let him go.

"Look at me, filth." It wasn't Willa's voice brimming with rage.

A male stood just inside the bubble prison, hands clenched into fists. He wore the same sort of bubble garment as Willa over his lean build. And he strode forward fists clenched. "I knew I should have killed you. Knew you would never help her."

Mathis pushed himself up off the floor, his instincts screaming that he needed to be on his feet, in his cougar aspect to fight the new threat. But his hand still throbbed from the scald when he'd attacked Willa. Would it protect this male the same way.

"Samantha Sinclair is mine by right of our birth. I am to be her king consort and rule our great city. Yet she's more concerned with avenging one of the animals she's been bedding."

He sneered and Mathis growled low in instinctive response. Fuck it, he'd bum rush the prick and shift mid stride. If the bubble did retaliate his thick coat would protect him.

"Guardian," The male's lips twisted in an evil smile.

And another being formed inside the bubble.

"Drag the shifter out into the depths. And this time, don't allow it to breathe."

CHAPTER 22
SAM

We all crowded inside Blinky because none of us trusted Willa not to make a run for it the way Wade had.

"He's obsessed with the princess," Willa confessed. "Has been following her for years, looking for a way to lure her to Atlantis. Calls himself her secret admirer. He believes it's his destiny to save her and usher in a new era for the Collective."

She didn't look directly at me as she spoke. Probably a good thing since the thought of her with Mathis made me want to rip her red hair out and stuff it down her pale throat.

"I see a couple of problems with that plan," Ginny, ever logical said." One, if he admires Sam so much why not tell her directly? Why all the games?"

"She's always been with someone else," Willa said. "First Damien then when he went back years later, she was married to another man who according to reports, treated her poorly."

Bile rose in my throat at the thought of someone knowing what Robert had done to me. And the stark reality that if Wade had revealed himself then, I might have been desperate enough to transfer my affections from my abusive husband to the megalomaniacal siren. Instead, he left me to wither under Robert.

"He said her ordeals on land would make her an even stronger queen," Willa babbled.

"Except she isn't the queen," Eric pointed out. "Not unless something happens to Caspian, right?"

Silence.

"Oh come on, he planned to kill my mate and my father?" I snapped. "And he really thought I would chose him as a consort after pulling that shit?"

"It wouldn't be a choice," Caspian said softly.

"What?"

He shook his head. "By the contract that I signed if you ever came to Atlantis and were unmated, Wade would be your consort and rule by your side."

I blew out a breath. "Look, Cas. I don't know how you've been doing things under the sea, but—"

"Look!" Ginny pointed out Blinky's view screen. I gaped as I took in the scene before us. One of the elementals hovered just outside an independent bubble that sat beside a larger bubble. The Siren's laboratory. The elemental had a white glow around it.

"That's the one," I breathed and then squinted. "What's it doing?"

The thing was reaching inside the bubble as though grasping at something, trying to tug it forth.

"Why didn't it come when you called them all to you?" I asked Caspian.

"It should have. Unless you and Wade found a way to free an elemental from my control?"

Judging by the look on the siren's downcast eyes, that was exactly what she'd done.

Pressing Blinky's joystick so that I would come up behind the elemental I kept my gaze on the scene. And gasped when a Cougar's beefy tail emerged from the bubble, clutched within the elemental's watery fists.

"He's not shielded?" Willa surged forward.

"What does that mean?" I looked up at her. "If that thing yanks him out of the bubble he'll drown?"

Caspian laid a hand on my arm. "Outside Atlantis and our outlying structures, at this depth, the pressure will crush him first."

MATHIS'S CLAWS scrabbled on the floor, trying desperately to sink into something, anything that would hold him within the bubble. He'd shifted the moment the elemental had come for him, intending to fight the thing. But a swipe of his claws had proven useless. They cut through the being without harming it.

This was it. He'd known when he first beheld the thing that it meant death. He wanted to fight. So that at least his mate knew he fought for her. And for Damien.

That he didn't give up, even when the ending was inevitable.

Another yank from the elemental sent him skidding further. The wall that had been solid had somehow become permeable. He spared a killing look at the siren who'd summoned the creature. If not for his presence, it probably would have dissolved the structure entirely, letting the ocean crush him.

Yet another pull, and he felt one of his back feet slide outside the dome. The pressure compressed the bones and muscles immediately. He roared at the impact, the panther's cry of pain.

It felt as though the whole structure rocked. His gaze again went to the siren male. Instead of the look of triumph he'd sported seconds earlier, he now appeared, startled. As though something wasn't going to plan.

"I vow she will come to me unencumbered."

A bubble formed around him the second before something crashed through the far side of the sphere. Its pulsing green light flashed over the interior of the prison. The siren male floated up through the ceiling an instant before the hatch from the thing that had broken through his prison's barrier like the Kool-Aid Man through a brick wall began to open.

Oh, yeah.

The tugging on his foot had ceased. Had the elemental been called off?

Exhausted from his desperate fight, from the pain of his burn and the foot that was nothing but a white-hot ball of agony, Mathis tried to crawl back into the bubble. But that last little bit of exertion was too much and his eyes rolled back in his head the instant a set of familiar hands caught his face.

Sam

"Mathis?" I petted his fur, even as my magic flared out along his body, hunting for injury so I could heal him. He had a bad burn on one of his front feet and the back leg along with his tail had been pulverized by its time outside the bubble. "Eric, help me get him to Blinky."

The other shifter surged forward and picked up the cougar with his superhuman strength. He carried him up into the ship and I lurched to follow.

"That was extremely reckless," Caspian said as I came up the gangway. "You had no idea if the bubble would hold or if the hull of your biomechanoid would be breached."

I stared at him for a long moment. Even though the urge to go to Mathis, to Heal him was almost overwhelming I had to say this. "You're right, I didn't. That's the sort of shit you do for people you love. You make sacrifices. But I guess that didn't ever occur to you."

His snowy brows drew together. "Samantha?"

"Did you know mom took part of the Siren's curse into herself? She tried to take *it from me into herself.* So I would survive. I would do the same for Damien, for Mathis, for John or Emily. That's love." My bottom lip quivered as I said. "You don't know the meaning of the word."

Screw Caspian and screw Atlantis. I'd lived over five decades without them. I could live the rest of my life without them. I'd survive.

Sniffling, I fell to my knees beside Mathis, my white light emerging from my hands as I focused first on his foot and tail and then moved up to that burn. I was so focused on what I was doing that it barely registered when Eric said. 'Uh oh. we've got company and they don't look happy."

I glanced out of Blinky's rear viewscreen to see what looked like a legion of sirens encased in bubbles, weapons at the ready.

"What is this?" Caspian snarled.

"Insurrection," Willa murmured. "Wade had it in place. They were supposed to turn on Caspian at the banquet, take his head and end his reign but no one expected you to interfere."

My heart lurched. "Take his head?"

"It's our way," Willa said with a chilling blankness. "The transfer of power can only occur after the regent dies."

"Yes," Wrath purred inside me. The bloodthirsty bitch reveled in the idea of a *coup d'état*.

My lips parted as I looked at Caspian. "I don't want it. I refuse to take it."

He removed the pearl cuff from his arm and placed it on mine. "Go, I'll buy you as much time as I can."

Before anyone could say anything, he let out one solid note and disappeared.

"Whoa," Eric breathed. "He freaking ghosted through the walls."

Indeed, he had. In his own bubble, Caspian faced off alone against the army that descended on us. More bubbles formed around him, layers upon layers of them.

Mathis was still unconscious and would probably stay that way for several hours. I gave the screen my full attention. "What's happening?"

"They're firing something at him," Ginny said.

"No," I snarled. Damn it, I'd just gone full bitch-kitty on Caspian. If he died now, I'd never be able to take it back.

"Eric," I said. "Drive forward,"

"What's the plan, matriarch?" The shifter asked. There was a scraping sound as Blinky continued to roll forward through the prison only to break free on the far side. We pitched down, but I imagined a bubble around the vehicle to slow our descent.

Eric turned so we were heading toward Caspian.

I stumbled forward just as the first beam of.... *something*, rippled past our bubble. "What was that?"

Eric checked the viewscreen where Blinky was demonstrating the schematics for some weapons. He had his translation glasses back on and was scowling at the display. "According to this it's a sonic weapon."

"Sonic?" Made sense considering they were Sirens and voice was their weapon of choice. "Will it really do any harm?"

The last syllable had left my mouth just as another

wavering blast ricocheted off Caspian's bubble. It was redirected into the larger dome behind us.

The research station's bubble burst. The pressure from the sea rushed in to fill the vacuum, pulverizing the laboratory.

"No!" Willa shrieked. Her lips quivered as she beheld the wreckage. She appeared, lost. I would have felt sorry for her but then she said, "All my work, all that research. Gone."

"Were there people in there?" I asked.

She didn't answer just shook her head.

"How close is the portal?" I asked Willa.

She lifted her chin to a defiant angle. The truth serum had worn off.

"Fine," I snarled and blew the knockout powder into her eyes.

She swayed and then toppled over beside Mathis.

"Sam!" Eric shouted. "If you have a plan, now's the time to let me know what it is. I don't want to be on the receiving end of one of those things."

"The plan is to grab Caspian and beat feet for the portal." I snatched the bubble ring off Willa's finger. She too had control over the same elemental as Wade.

"Grab him how?"

"Still working on that part." I leaned over the controls. "Blinky, can you give me an inventory list of all your functions and equipment on board."

The list came up on two screens. Ginny, translation readers already in place gripped one and I focused on the other.

"Anything?"

I was about to say no when I spotted it. "There. Blinky, give me this on my mark."

The biomechanoid churred.

Whatever strength Caspian had in his bubble layers was beginning to fail. A direct hit cracked the outer layer of his first bubble.

Eric navigated in behind him, using Caspian's shield to keep any of those blasts from hitting him.

"Why doesn't he call the elementals?" Ginny asked.

"I don't know." Then I looked down at the pearl bracelet he'd thrust at me before he'd disappeared. "Oh, shit. Gin."

"What?"

"Nothing." I didn't know how to make the sound Caspian had. How to summon the elementals. He would need to teach me.

The last of Caspian's outer bubbles burst when we were about ten meters behind him. He slumped, the only thing keeping him alive the small personal bubble.

"Now, Blinky!" I shouted.

A golden net shot out, landing over Caspian as Eric banked hard down below the army.

"Got him!" The shifter growled as Blinky's net trailed along.

I decided to take a page out of Caspian's book. In my mind, I formed several more bubbles around Blinky and the net we were dragging. I had no illusion they'd hold up to the onslaught from the sonic weapons, but they were better than nothing.

"Gin, a location spell. You need to find that portal," I demanded.

"On it." She pulled her scrying crystal off from around her neck and began to chant.

"They've stopped firing!" Eric called.

"What?" I looked up at the screen. He was right. Though the siren's gave chase they'd quit firing at us. "Why?"

"They don't want to risk you, Sam."

I whirled around, saw Caspian had transported himself back inside. After the battle, he appeared much closer to his age. "You're their queen."

"You mean, I'm supposed to be Wade's puppet." I shoved the bracelet underneath his nose. "Tell me how to use this."

"Your heart song will invoke it, allow you to command the guardians." His eyes rolled up in his head and he passed out.

Heart song? That was the noise he made? I had no idea how to replicate it.

"Found the portal," Ginny said. Her scrying crystal was horizontal to the ground and pointing to our left. "Northwest, Eric. On the far side of the city."

"Sam?"

I turned and saw Mathis had his eyes cracked open. With a cry I went to him. "Hey, evil twin. I've got you. I'm taking you home."

Instead of relief I saw panic on his face. "You have to hurry."

"What? Why?"

My blood chilled when he said, "That siren and his elemental are going to kill Damien."

CHAPTER
TWENTY-THREE

Damien paced the interior of Mel's bar. "There has to be something we can do?"

"The best offense is a solid defense," Jim said. "We need to find a way to protect the community from the elementals."

"Do you suggest anything specific, Jim?" Fran asked.

Jim hesitated. "We could ask the demon."

"No," Damien's snarl was immediate. "That creature upset and distressed Sam. She cut her ties to it, and I will not let it back into our community."

"Think this through, Damien." Sally put her hand on his shoulder. "The Demon is the only one of us with strong enough magic to make a difference against something like an elemental."

"But demons are as bad as the fey. It'll want to bargain with us." And Damien feared the thing would want something he'd regret.

Mel and Javier exchanged a glance. "I'm not sure we have much of a choice, boss." The true shifter said. "We need to consider either evacuating or asking the demon for an assist."

Bea lifted her chin to a stubborn angle. "I vote we evacuate. One small stretch of beach isn't worth all our lives."

"I won't leave Sam," Damien said. "If there is any chance at all that Mathis is still alive, I want to be as close to them as possible. If any of you want to go, you can."

No one budged, not even Bea. They were a community, a group. They would have each other's backs.

"Fine then." Damien rose to his full height. "I'll talk to the demon."

He only hoped he wouldn't regret it.

The Investor stood in the doorway of the B&B. The sight of the demon presiding over the place where his mother had once stood made his hackles rise.

Let it go. Damien told himself. For the community. For Mathis and Sam, he would let his bitterness ebb.

"Mr. Moss. I've noticed you haven't been going to your restaurant of late." The demon said in a blasé tone. "Family problems not resolving?"

Though every word felt like it was being pulled from him with a grappling hook Damien managed to grate, "We...need your help."

The demon's lips twitched. "Is that so? And are you here to make a bargain?"

He nodded once.

"Fine." The demon twirled his cane. "What exactly is it that you need my help with shifter?"

"I need to know if there's any way to stop an

elemental."

Interest sparked in the demon's dark eyes. "And in exchange for this information you will offer me...?" He raised one eyebrow and waited.

Damien licked suddenly dry lips. "Whatever you want."

"Oh, Mr. Moss, you are nowhere near as clever as your mate. You're fortunate I've turned over a new leaf or I wouldn't hesitate to take shameless advantage of your pathetic desperation."

Damien waited.

"I have pressing business in the mountains and Samantha's rather abrupt departure has left me short-staffed. In exchange for the knowledge you seek, members of your community will continue to run this property for me successfully for the next, five years."

"One year," Damien responded.

The demon tut-tutted him. "Oh, shifter it is far too late for haggling. I already know you're desperate. Honestly, Samantha Sinclair can do so much better than you."

"Fine," Damien held out a hand. "It's a bargain."

"A bargain well struck." The Investor wrapped his creepy long fingers around Damien's, and he felt the surge of magic flow between them.

"There is no way to kill an elemental." The demon said.

Damien's jaw dropped. "You tricked me?"

Another raised eyebrow look. "I'm a demon, Mr. Moss. We're not exactly known for our generous natures. As it happens though, no, I didn't. You asked me if there was a way to stop an elemental. I said there's no way to kill it. To stop it, you need to summon one of its ilk to drag it back to whence it came. This will free the creature from whatever compulsion it's been put under. A mystical reboot if you will."

Damien swallowed and nodded. His mother had taught him to never thank a fae and Damien decided that was good advice for demons as well. "I appreciate your assistance."

He turned to sprint across the highway when the demon called, "I'll expect one of you first thing in the morning!"

Damien was halfway down the dune when he saw it.

A creature made entirely of water heading straight for him.

"That siren," Mathis struggled to sit up. "He wants Damien dead."

Blinky shook as we rumbled through the portal, only to be spat out by the Monitor's wreck. There was no sign of the elemental that had guided us to Atlantis. Had it been summoned away from his post with the rest when Caspian had called?

Ginny handed me a blanked and I wrapped it around Mathis. I hoped he wasn't going into shock. His whole body trembled. "He regrets not killing me. He said he would free you."

Wade had a head start. And who knew how fast an elemental could travel? I shut my eyes and felt along the familiar bond, trying to warn Damien. Nothing. We were too far apart. We were hours away from the Convergence at the rate Blinky traveled.

"Caspian," I shook his shoulder. A quick probe with my Healer's light told me he was all right, just exhausted.

Heart song, he'd said. What was my heart's song?

Mathis's dark gaze fell on the still-unconscious Willa. His teeth bared in a snarl.

I caught him around the waist before he could lunge for her. "Easy."

"You wouldn't stop me if you knew what she wanted," he growled. "What she wanted

me to do."

"Is there any chance she might be pregnant?" I didn't want to ask, but I needed to.

He turned away from the unconscious siren and looked at me. "Not by me."

I could see all he didn't say in the depth of his dark gaze. Even without the familiar bond I knew the thoughts racing through his mind. He'd considered it, feared what I would think because he'd been weak.

I kissed him on the forehead, a benediction I could bestow that might bring him some peace. "Not your fault, Mathis. No matter what, I don't blame you for any of it. And even if you had been with her, it wouldn't change my love for you."

He drew in a shuddering breath and crushed me to him. "My mate."

I swallowed. "She told me she broke the bond."

"Doesn't matter." Mathis rocked me gently. "I'll find some other way to tether you to me. There's no getting away, little witch."

I allowed myself the span of several heartbeats to just hold him. I wanted to fall apart in his arms. To confess how horrible it had been thinking he was dead, how I wanted to destroy the elemental, the whole city of Atlantis for taking him from me. Mathis would understand.

But I couldn't fall apart yet. Damien was in danger. I needed to figure out how to use the damn cuff to control the elementals.

"They're still following us," Eric said.

I pulled back and looked. It appeared as if the entire city of Atlantis had crossed the portal and dogged Blinky. Would they follow us all the way to the beach?

"Options," I asked my friend. "No matter how nutty, let's hear them."

As much of a problem as the contingent of sirens was, I was more concerned with the elemental. Once again, I asked myself, how did you fight an unstoppable being?

"You could give the cuff back to Caspian," Ginny suggested.

It was an option. But not only was he unconscious, he had bestowed the thing to me. Despite his show of sacrifice, I didn't trust him, not with Damien's life on the line. The sirens were as cold as the water they lived in.

"He said something about a heart song," I told them. "But I have no idea what that is."

Eric and Mathis shook their heads, though Ginny frowned. "Sam, do you recall the song you sang Damien when you were healing him from his head injury at all?"

"No. I didn't even realize I was singing at all until you said something about it."

She smiled and nodded. "That's it then. The song that flows from your heart, which gives you comfort."

"But how can I access it?" I asked. Always with music I listened and drew the melody, the lyrics into myself. "I have no idea how to tap into it."

"We can try a regression spell," Ginny said. "You got this, hon?" She asked Eric.

He nodded. "Do what you do, babe."

"Mathis, I need you to shift." Avoiding Caspian and Willa's inert form, Ginny sank gracefully to the floor.

Mathis released me and dropped the blanket. A moment later the cougar stood beside me, his newly repaired tail slowly swishing.

"Sit," Ginny commanded.

I sat and the cougar pressed up against my knee.

"I'm going to bring you into a hypnotic state," The green witch said as she held her scrying crystal aloft. I expected her to swing it back and forth and murmur something like "You are getting sleepy." Obviously, I watch too much trash TV.

Instead, Ginny spun the crystal on the chain. "Look at it, Sam and let your gaze go unfocused."

I did as she commanded. Paying attention to the way the crystal caught and reflected the green glow of Blinky's running lights.

I hadn't realized I'd sagged into the cougar until he

was right there beside me, acting as my pillow.

"How do you feel?" Ginny asked.

"Comfortable." There was nothing like having a cougar for a pillow.

"Good. Now I want you to remember something, Sam. You are safe here. Nothing can hurt you right now. Now, how do you feel?"

"Safe," I breathed.

"Very good. Now focus on the crystal and while you do that, think back to the other night when Damien was hurt. We're in your bedroom and his head is bleeding. Your hands are glowing and you're looking down at your mate, trying to Heal him with your magic. Can you see it?"

"Yes." The scene was vivid in my mind. All my focus was on helping Damien.

"How do you feel?" Ginny asked.

"Angry. He's hurt. He drove himself home. Something hurt him." Wrath tried to surge up inside me and I stiffened.

"It's okay to be angry, Sam." Ginny's voice floated as if it were carried on a breeze. "Someone you loved got hurt. So be angry about that."

"I can't," my voice came out like a whimper. "Can't let her loose."

"Her who?"

I shook my head, squeezing my eyes shut.

"You're safe. Everyone is safe. Take a deep breath." Ginny retrenched. "Okay. Let's go back to another time when you felt the same way."

My lids lifted and the crystal glinted, lulling me back

under her spell. When had I felt Wrath before that night? With contractors. With doctors, but that was different. I'd been angry but never tempted to release the monstrous entity inside of me. Not even with Robert.

"When Ray died," I breathed.

"Tell me about that. Where are you?"

"Standing by his grave." My throat felt thick, clogged with tears.

"And is she there?" Ginny asked.

I nodded. "I'm too weak. Too drained. All alone. She seizes on my weakness. I can't hold her down."

"Sam, I want you to draw her out. Like venom from a wound, let her out in whatever form she comes to you."

I shook my head against the cougar, but it was no use. I had no defense against the feeling. Wrath emerged from my throat in a mournful tune.

Ginny said nothing as I sang, a death dirge, mourning my beloved brother. It was a melody without words, it was all of me poured into the notes. Everything I was or would ever be emerged in that song. Angry, protective, destructive.

But also nurturing, intelligent and accepting of those around me. On and on and on it went until finally the last note faded.

My heart's song.

Beneath me the cougar began to growl.

"Sam," Ginny said in a much different tone.

When I opened my eyes a watery being crouched over me. It's sightless eyes inquiring. Behind it, more had crowded into Blinky's cabin.

"Well, hello there," I said to the elemental.

CHAPTER
TWENTY-FOUR

Damien sprinted toward the bar even as the watery being charged up the beach for him. Heart in his throat, he debated shifting and luring the thing away from the rest of his people. Before he could make the call, the creature had transformed into a mighty wave and knocked him flat.

Sputtering, Damien slashed out with his claws. They cut through watery hands that clamped down on him. The being lifted him as easily as he lifted Emily and threw him over its shoulder.

Damien fought but just like Mathis there was nothing he could do to prevent the elemental from taking him wherever it intended. He roared in frustration, letting the pack know what was happening.

Moments later a hippopotamus barreled through the wall of the bar. Mel. Javier was right behind them, a shotgun that was most likely loaded for bear trained on the elemental. He wouldn't fire unless Damien was clear.

The hippo charged them, mouth wide. Damien

shifted, uncaring that his clothing shredded beneath his magic. He stood a better chance in his cougar aspect. An instant before the true shifter went through them, the elemental dissipated, water droplets absorbed into the sand.

Damien surged out of the way a heartbeat before Mel ran him down. He ran for all he was worth, trying to get clear, to give Javier a shot.

Out of the corner of his eye he spied a man standing at the water's edge. He didn't smell human, nor did he smell like any being Damien had ever encountered. Was that the being controlling the elemental? If so, Damien would do his level best to take it out before the watery being destroyed him. He altered his course, gunning for the stranger.

Jim, Sally, Fran, Ivan, and Bea all stood on the deck. They must have noticed his altered course. The five coven members held hands and magic swirled around their heads.

A blast of magic surged forth and bounced off an invisible shield. Behind Damien the report of a shotgun sounded. He doubted bullets would even slow the elemental down but perhaps Mel and Javier could keep the water being busy long enough for Damien to take out the man.

He prepared to launch himself into the man, aiming to rip his throat out. When the other man opened his mouth and sang...

All the large muscles in Damien's body froze. Behind him, the sound of battle ceased. The stranger was controlling them all with the sound of his voice.

With a splash the elemental reformed behind the stranger.

And Damien knew he was about to die.

My throat had gone dry as I stared up into the elemental's face. Because of Mathis's experience, I'd believed these beings were evil. But they weren't.

I'd misjudged Wrath, thinking that my siren half was pure evil. I wouldn't make that same mistake twice.

They were enslaved to the sirens. And one was being used to do things that were against its very nature. These creatures were protectors of mother earth and all her gifts to the living beings, not errand boys for a lazy, fearful society.

I'd intended to send the elementals after Wade. But after looking one of them in its face and seeing intelligence there I knew what I had to do.

Out of my pocket, I pulled a small vial of dirt. Grave dirt, from Alba's grave. Tugging the siren's bracelet off my arm I laid it on the deck and then sprinkled the dirt over it.

"Rest," I commanded the beings, using Wrath's siren song.

The pearl bracelet disintegrated.

For one terrifying moment I believed that I had made a horrible mistake. Would the newly freed beings pull blinky apart in retribution for all that had been done to them?

But then they vanished much the same way Caspian had.

"Look!" Eric pointed out one of Blinky's viewscreens.

A whirlpool was forming between us and the pursuing sirens. The vortex expanded until it began engulfing the bubbles.

"Holy shit." Mathis had transformed back to his human form and had come to stand behind me. "Did that really just happen?"

"What are they doing now? Ginny asked.

I let out a shaky breath and leaned into him. Several of the elementals had moved in front of us and created yet another whirlpool.

"Should I aim for it?" Eric looked at our faces.

"I think they're trying to help us." I looked at Mathis. "What do you think?"

"You just did them a solid, little witch." He clapped his brother on the shoulder. "Full steam ahead Mr. Crusher."

At my puzzled look Ginny said, "Star Trek, The Next Generation. Surely you know what massive Sci-fi geeks these two are."

"I didn't," I said even as Mathis blushed. "Secret shame, evil twin?"

Eric, who was utterly shameless, laughed. "It's good to have you back, bro. No one gets as riled as you."

He pressed Blinky's joystick forward and we rolled through the portal. Again, the reverberation felt as though it was about to pull us apart. Mathis pressed me up against one wall, using his bodyweight to keep me from going flying as the biomechanoid shook and jounced through the rift.

When we emerged, it was onto dry land. Blinky shot forward as though jet propelled. And up ahead we spotted the convergence.

"Oh, my goddess," Ginny breathed.

Wade, faced off against the coven. Damien stood poised for attack as the elemental bore down on him.

"Open the hatch, Blinky!" I shouted.

The door behind me began to lower. Mathis pulled away long enough to shift once more. I climbed onto his back and the second he could we rushed out.

A splash beside us told me that one of the elementals had followed.

A surge of joy flowed through the familiar bond as Damien caught sight of us. A word flitted along the current, underscored in red panic.

Another.

What did that mean? And then the question I'd asked myself before registered. How do you stop an unstoppable being.

With another unstoppable being.

Realization dawned. Another elemental could stop the one Wade had taken over.

"Can you stop it?" I asked the wave that surged just behind us. "Can you free that one too?"

There was no verbal communication. But the wave dissipated. We ran on and I opened my mouth, sending out a pure, clear note to free my friends from Wade's influence.

Princess's Heart Song trumped social climbing dickheads. Damien charged Wade, knocking the startled siren back into the surf. Another elemental rose behind the one that had been looming over Damien and then both were dragged down into the ocean as though caught in a riptide.

The stories were right. Elementals were the good guys. Anything wretched they'd been forced to do because they'd been in service to the sirens.

We charged up beside Damien where he stood on top of Wade, teeth bared in obvious threat. The siren's frantic gaze went to mine. "Samantha, please. Have mercy."

"How much mercy have you shown any of us?" I asked Wade.

He whimpered in fright as Damien snapped his jaws inches from his face.

"You watched me for years. Never helping, never approaching, just waiting for a chance to take something from me." My voice shook. "Give me one good reason why I shouldn't let the pack pull you apart?"

Wade's gray eyes filled with panic. "Don't. Please," he moaned.

"You can't can you? You haven't done one decent thing in your entire existence that would speak for your character. You've plotted for power you don't deserve and based on this whole thing, would most definitely abuse."

Another terrified whimper.

"Take his head," Wrath whispered. *"He deserves no better."*

I sighed to that bloodthirsty part of me, *"Maybe not, but I do."*

Out loud I said, "Damien, let him up."

The cougar looked over his shoulder at me and bared his teeth.

"I mean it." I said, using the familiar and pack bonds to emphasize my point.

With a final sneer down at the siren, Damien backed off. Wade surged to his feet and stumbled back, The bubble formed around him and he dove beneath the waves.

Damien and Mathis moved to stop him.

"Let him go." I slid off Mathis's back and watched as a wave built and built. For one moment I saw faces in the water, No longer blank. Then the wave broke right atop the siren's head. There was a single scream that got cut off halfway. Then nothing. Wade disappeared beneath the waves where he would face whatever justice the elementals doled out.

A moment later I was wrapped in a double embrace of two naked shifters. "Guys, ease off." I laughed.

"No," Mathis rumbled even as Damien vowed, "Never."

My lips curved into a satisfied smile. "I can live with that."

Mel had made a mess of their bar. Damien and Mathis studied the hippopotamus-sized hole while I sat at the bar with Ginny and Eric.

"Why a hippopotamus?" Eric asked Mel.

The true shifter shrugged. "I was going for big and mean. Plus hippos are aquatic."

I put my hand over theirs. "Thank you, Mel. For charging to the rescue."

"Anything for the boss. Besides, I've been trying to convince Javier to put a bay window in for ages. So this works."

"You're really a siren?" Javier asked.

"Not to mention a princess," Eric added.

I swore and slid off the stool. Mathis and Damien were beside me in a hot minute.

"What is it, firecracker?" Damien asked.

"Caspian and Willa. I forgot all about them."

"Oh no worries," Ginny's tone was smug. "We took care of them."

"In like a mob way?" I asked.

"No as in a we sent Blinky back to the goblin queen with our thanks kinda way. Another dose of the forgetting powder for each of them inside." Eric clapped his brother on the shoulder. "It seemed like the least we could do to thank them for all they've done to you guys."

Mathis put a hand on top of his brother's and squeezed.

Walking stick in one hand and a rum and coke in the other, I headed out to the deck. The sun was behind the bar, casting me in shadow. I shivered when the wind blew off the ocean.

What had the elementals done to Wade? Would the rest of the sirens in Atlantis be all right now that I'd freed their providers?

I decided to do my best Scarlett O'Hara impression. Those were things I'd worry about tomorrow.

I felt his presence even before I saw his long lanky form crossing the sand. "John?"

"Hey, Mama. I was worried about you." My son ran lightly up the steps and drew me into his embrace.

I sagged into him, glad for his support. I hadn't realized how much I'd missed him. "Where's Emily? And Jessica?"

"At home. I didn't know what kind of epic shit you had going down here so I figured better for the two of them to hang back until I got the lay of the land."

I brushed some of his dark hair away from his piercing blue eyes. I'd always thought they were Damien's eyes but now I saw some of his grandfather there too.

I had mixed feelings regarding Caspian. While Willa deserved whatever the goblin queen decided to dish out, I wasn't convinced that the siren king—my father—was evil.

That was why Ginny and Eric had made the command decision. So I wouldn't feel guilty about it.

"Son!" Damien had spotted him through the hippo hole and charged out to wrap him in his embrace. Mathis followed more carefully, the reserve he had around John falling over him like a veil. I swallowed and reached out a hand for him.

John released his father with a slap on the back and

then, much to everyone's astonishment, gave Mathis the same sort of hug. I heard him murmur, "Glad you're not dead, man."

After a long moment, Mathis's face relaxed and he hugged John back with a ferocity he rarely showed to anyone aside from me and Damien. "That makes two of us."

"Three." I had tears in my eyes and snuffled. Then made to step back. Though my balance was off. Damien caught me with ease. "You okay, love?"

What a loaded question. I was back with my family, safe on dry land. And my MS symptoms/ siren curse symptoms had returned. Not with vengeance. I was no worse than when John had brought me here.

Would I trade all that I had, my son, my lovers, and friends for easy mobility? Never. Much like my mother, I would sacrifice for the people who lived in my heart.

Eric and Ginny had come up and along with Mathis were giving me knowing looks.

"It's better than it was," I addressed them. Mathis's shoulders relaxed. A bit.

"What am I missing?" Damien asked.

I put a hand on his arm and smiled. "I promise, I'll tell you everything later. Right now, I just want to enjoy being with all of you. Maybe we can have a karaoke night, though the acoustics are going to suck!"

"Bite me, matriarch!" Mel hollered back.

I caught Mathis's eye. "One thing first."

"What's that, little witch?"

I took Damien's hand in mine and offered the other

to Mathis. "I really need some help getting out of this dress. If I have any volunteers—hey!"

Damien had picked me up and tossed me over his shoulder. Mathis shifted and was charging ahead. Probably to get the shower up to the right temperature.

Home sweet home.

Just as I'd thought, Mathis had the shower running by the time Damien carried me over the threshold. Wally and Wilma leapt down from the couch and did victory zoomies around the living room.

"Hey babies," I cooed at the corgis. Damien set me down just outside the steamy bathroom, his brilliant blue eyes hot as they traveled from me to Mathis and back.

"I'll just go get the dogs settled for the night." Damien excused himself.

Mathis drew me against him. "You've been wearing this the whole time?"

I nodded, my throat thick with emotion. "I made you a promise. And I couldn't...I refused to let you go."

We'd thought he was dead, drowned by an elemental.

He began purring even as his lips traveled down my neck, His fingers settled over the zipper. I held my breath as he toyed with the small pull.

Yet he hesitated. "This isn't right."

Huh? "Feels right to me."

He cupped my shoulders and held me as he turned me to face him. "I can't feel you in my head anymore, little witch. I want to be your familiar again. I'm so pissed that they took that from us."

My fingers threaded through his. "You want me to rebind you as my familiar?"

He nodded and then glanced to the door where Damien stood. "Only...could you bond me to Damien, too?"

Damien looked as though he'd been struck by lightning. "You really want that?"

Mathis nodded fervently. "I want the three of us bound together in every way. I can

reestablish the pack bonds and I have no doubt the mating bond will come back as well. But I want that bridge to both your minds. If you want that?" He gazed hesitantly at Damien.

Damien's eyes glistened and he rasped, "Yeah, I want that."

"Okay then," I huffed. "Go shut off the shower before we run out of hot water. I need to think about the best way to do this."

Mathis flushed guiltily. "I didn't realize—"

I covered his mouth with my hand. "No apologizing. You are always supposed to tell us what you want and never apologize for that. I just need to consider how best to do this before I dive face first into a pool with no water. Besides, I'm happily unemployed now so it's not like I have an early morning."

Damien winced. "About that...."

Fifteen minutes later, I sat on the living room floor, still in my ruined silver dress with an unlit cinnamon candle and three rose quartz crystals placed in front of each of us. "I can't believe you bargained with that damned demon again. I do not want to work for him!"

"You don't have to," Damien said. "Mathis and I can do it."

Mathis raised his hand meekly. "Technically, I still work for the B&B. So does Eric so I'm betting we won't count."

"And you have a restaurant to run," I seethed. Damn it, I was supposed to be casting a freaking binding love spell and instead I was nail-spitting mad.

Mathis circled around the coffee table and began rubbing my shoulders. "Easy little witch. No need to lose your cool right now. We'll figure it all out."

"*I'll* figure it out. You got yourself kidnapped because you didn't follow the buddy rule and he made the worst bargain ever. Five years, really Damien?"

The tips of his ears turned red. "Hey, we needed the information. And I'm sure the others will help."

I closed my eyes and drew in a deep breath. "I just wasn't expecting to ever go back there. I need a minute to process."

I felt Damien crawl closer and heard his easy purr. He took my left hand in his and brought it to his lips for a soft kiss before murmuring, "Forgive me."

When my eyes opened his soft lips were inches away from my face, driving me to distraction "You know I always do. Now back in place, both of you. I have a spell to do."

They obeyed. It was a waxing crescent moon. A good time for planting new seeds. The traditional verbiage for a familiar bond was to recite the vow, *You belong to me. Body mind, and spirit. You will give your all.* Then the familiar would recite it back to the witch in acceptance of her authority and together we would light the candle.

Feeling my way along my familiar bond with Damien, I decided I would rework this new bond a little for all our benefit. Picking up my athame, I drew a casting circle with my energy, then took up my crystal.

"We belong to each other. Body, mind, and spirit. We will give our all."

I looked to Damien first, since our bond was still intact. He held his own crystal over his heart and repeated the vow, meeting my gaze, a smile tugging at the corner of his mouth. Mathis followed suit much more solemnly and then each of us reached for the long-handled matches next to the candle.

When the head of my matchstick was lit I held it a scant inch above the pristine wick. "On three we light the wick together. One."

Damien held his match at an angle to mine directly above the candle. "Two."

"Three." Mathis added his flame to ours and three small fires burned brighter as they ignited the cinnamon candle.

Outside on the porch I heard the wind gusting and the seashell chimes clinging. And then power swept through the room, through our circle. I drew a deep breath...feeling, feeling, feeling there. I felt them. My shifters. My loves.

From my end, I could always see both of their thoughts so I had to ask, "Did it work? Can you feel each other?"

Damien's lips parted and he was staring at Mathis with an expression close to amazement "I can feel you."

Mathis nodded, though the emotion drifting along the newly forged link was hesitant. "It's not exactly like it was before but I can feel you both."

Damien gasped and clutched his head.

"What?" I asked. "Is there pain?"

"Just trying to sort through it all." Then he glared at Mathis. "How could you ever think

we'd be okay without you?"

I shivered as I experienced the gray desolation Mathis had felt when he'd been abducted and that siren had tried to convince him Damien and I wouldn't miss him. "You know better than that. We love you, idiot."

Giddiness radiated out of Mathis's bond as his mind reached for me a moment before his arms did. "Thank you, little witch," he breathed into my hair.

I held him for all I was worth and then said briskly. "Now, will someone please help me out of this fucking dress before it becomes a permanent part of me?"

Damien and Mathis exchanged a grin.

"That can be arranged, little witch."

Need more witch-on-shifter-on-shifter action in your life? Want to see the removal of Sam's silver dress and a more intimate reunion? Sign up for my author newsletter and get the Midlife Magic and Malarkey directrix's cut scene now!

NOTE FROM THE AUTHOR

Thank you so much for reading. The outpouring of love and acceptance for this series has been incredible. I really do have the best readers and I have so much fun crafting these little after-book notes for you as well as coming up with fun titles!

Speaking of which, did you know the word malarkey is not Irish in nature? That was always my impression. The word was actually coined by an Irish-American cartoonist in the early 20th century. Essentially it means "to talk nonsense." And what better word to use for a book about sirens?

I took some liberties with Sam's MS symptoms in this book. While I've always wanted to be true to the nature of chronic illness, spoonies, and the warriors who battle MS symptoms every day, for the sake of advancing the plot I added the siren's curse wrinkle. And hell, maybe all of those afflicted with MS are part mystical creatures with hidden powers that are supposed to dwell in a magical world beneath the waves. After all, there's

NOTE FROM THE AUTHOR

so much science doesn't know about the disease. Which in my mind translates to anything is possible!

So what's next? Well, I am glad you asked. I'm juggling three ongoing series. Be sure to check out my new series and meet Bella and Donna Sanders. You'll run into a very familiar demon in the Legacy Witches of Shadow Cove series. Book 1 *Midlife Magic Mirror* is available now with Book 2 *Midlife Magic Monster* slated for an early October release.

In December the final book in the Silver Sisters series *Witch Way Ever After,* and I plan to head back to the beach for more Cougars and Cauldrons in early 2024! All these dates are subject to change. To keep up with the latest sign up for my author newsletter.

Love and light,

Jennifer L. Hart

PS. Please consider leaving an honest review for *Midlife Magic and Malarkey.* Reviews help readers find the kind of books they're looking for and help authors get the word out. And even if you don't love it, that's okay too. I found one of my favorite series by reading a two-star review. (It said the book had too much sex, so I went, bingo, right for me!)

DIRECTRIX CUT SCENE

We headed into the bathroom and while Damien started the shower, Mathis smoothed my hair over one shoulder and finally, *finally*, tugged the zipper down. I sighed when it pooled around my feet.

I tipped my head back against his shoulders as he cupped my breasts through my strapless bra. He kissed along the exposed column of my throat as he toyed with my nipples.

"Please," I moaned.

"You ever going to wear this thing again?" Damien had come to stand in front of me, blue gaze hot.

"Not if I can help it."

Claws emerged and he sliced through the fabric and it fell away, my boobs spilled into his waiting palms.

"That feels so good," I moaned.

"Having the bra off or having Damien fondling you?" Mathis asked.

"Both."

The mirror fogged with steam as they touched my

body. Need for them was growing hotter, making me crave deeper touches. Mathis bit the tendon of my neck and I cried out. I wanted to sob as desire pooled low in my belly, liquifying my core and turning my bones to jelly.

Mathis scooped me up and carried me into the shower. After setting me down under the spray he stepped back, gesturing for Damien to take the spot in front of him. "I know you like to tend to her."

Damien nodded as we crammed into the overlarge shower. "Turn around, firecracker,"

I did though I caught Mathis's gaze over my shoulder while Damien busied himself with the shampoo. Evil twin nodded solemnly as though the picture I'd flashed him was an order he would dutifully obey.

I tipped my head back and allowed Damien to scrub my hair, combing through my tresses with his claws. "Never feels as good without my bath attendant," I murmured.

"You will never be without him again if I have anything to say about it." A soft kiss landed on my shoulder. "Turn around so I can rinse the suds out."

I pivoted to face him, then leaned back against the safety rail and tilted my head. "I've got a better idea."

Before he could answer Mathis had his hands around Damien's hard shaft, fisting it in a tight grip. Damien gasped, hips rocking into the touch as Mathis plastered himself against his back. They both stood there, frozen, hungry, waiting for the other to make a move.

"Did you really think we weren't going to see this

little fantasy?" I crooned "You have two mates inside your mind, now, Damien Moss."

"I...I..." he stuttered because Mathis had begun rocking his hips against him in tandem to pulling on his cock.

"Yeah, we know what you want," I told him. "You've both been thinking about it for a very long time."

"He didn't want to," Damien choked out. "I offered—"

"Want had nothing to do with it," Mathis bit Damien's earlobe as he rocked against him. "I needed to control something. And where my dick went was about the only thing I could control. That doesn't mean I didn't want you." His thumb glided over the leaking slit.

"The invisible lines you two drew aren't necessary anymore," I tipped my hair back into

the water, rinsing the suds down the drain. After wringing out the excess moisture, I reached for my body wash. "We're starting fresh, as equals."

Two sets of hot shifter gazes were on me as I suds up my arms and shoulders, my breasts and belly. I kept my focus on myself as the two of them explored each other's bodies even as they watched me. They didn't need an intermediary, but I would be a very happy spectator to their games.

Damien's hips began to jerk into Mathis's grip. Through the bond I felt waves of pleasure as he let his lover stroke his length, milking little glistening droplets from the tip of his cock.

Mathis spun Damien around so his back slammed into the far wall. I saw the mental image in his mind a moment before he backed up to where I was perched. My arms went around him and I crushed my breasts against his broad back even as I reached around him to clasp his thick cock that stood proud and hard and ready for more.

My gaze locked on Damien even as I murmured in Mathis's ear. "You want him on his knees, don't you?"

Twin groans filled the shower stall.

"I'll take that as a yes. Here, let me get him ready for you." I released Mathis and reached for the soap. Leisurely, I scrubbed his back, admiring his sculpted muscles. The dips and hollows beckoned to me and before I knew it I was humming to myself as I explored his hard body. Damien's gaze was glued to my movements as I worked my way down a well-muscled ass, taut thighs, and calves. I could feel Damien's heated gaze traveling over me, drinking it all in. Yet he didn't budge. Over Mathis's feet and then up the front of his legs I went with my sudsy palms. Mathis's lids were heavy and I nipped his hip playfully. I intentionally skipped his groin, moving on to his lower abdomen and up over his chest.

"So stubborn," I murmured as I pinched Mathis's nipples hard enough that he started. "The both of you. You both want this, but neither of you will break first. Damien, if I need to order you to suck him off, I'll fucking do it." I said it in my best, *don't make me back there*, tone.

Damien groaned.

Mathis chuckled darkly. "Easy, little witch. Keep talking filthy and he might drop dead of a coronary." But he took the hint and gripped his cock. "I think you missed a spot. Damien, would you—?"

DIRECTRIX CUT SCENE

The rest of the sentence was cut off on a hoarse cry as Damien fell to his knees and greedily sucked Mathis's thick length into his mouth. My lips parted and I readjusted my perch on the *oh, shit* bar so I could watch over Mathis's shoulder.

It was his turn to tip his head back. His mouth hung open and bliss flowed from his end of the bond.

"How does it feel?" I asked as I nipped his ear. "Having his mouth on you? His rough textured tongue. Is it as good as you imagined?"

"Better," he groaned.

My hands, now divested of soap, roamed over his body adding light stimulation to his skin. Damien reached up and sank his claws into Mathis ass, dragging him closer as though he feared Mathis would pull away.

"Are you gonna let him seize the upper hand like that?" I baited Mathis.

"Do you have a better suggestion?" He rasped.

"Yeah. Hold him still and fuck his mouth."

Air left his lungs in a rush. "Gods, Sam." Mathis grated even as pure need coursed through Damien's bond.

"You asked." My tone was pure innocence.

His fingers fisted in Damien's salt and pepper hair, forcing the other shifter to release him. Damien's glassy blue gaze focused on me a moment before Mathis rolled his hips forward and back, then forward and back. He bobbed up and down, taking Mathis so much deeper than I ever had, I ever could. The thought made me sad in a bittersweet way. At least they could do this for each other. They both paused.

"What?" Mathis turned to look at me over his shoulder. "What are you thinking about?"

I tried to wave it way. "It's nothing. As you were."

"It's not nothing." Damien rasped. "I felt this regretful pang coming from you, but I can't pinpoint what caused it."

Mathis reached behind me and shut off the shower. "Out with it, little witch. Part of what was doing it for me was feeling you taking pleasure in what we were doing."

Damien nodded, wincing as he regained his footing. His cock bobbed, as though seeking attention. "If something's changed we need to know."

The two of them would be dealing with an epic case of blue balls because I was feeling a little, well, blue? Fine if they were going to be stubborn, I might as well spill. "If you must know I felt a little sorry for myself for a moment because I can't do what Damien was doing. Physically I mean."

Blank stares.

Embarrassment had me snapping, "Okay, so if the water isn't running the shower isn't fun anymore. I'm getting out. You two can just finish each other up."

Before I could open the glass door, I was being pressed flat between two male bodies.

Damien's cheek rested on my head. "Are you saying you wish you could deep throat Mathis, firecracker?"

Gritting my teeth I said, "No, I'm saying I'm pissed that my goddamned MS or siren's curse or whatever keeps taking options off the table."

"Who says?" Mathis nuzzled my ear. He looked over

to Damien and I could tell they were sharing a mental image. Oh no. What were the two of them plotting?

Faster than I could track, Damien had snagged a pair of towels off the shelf just outside of the shower. Tossing one to Mathis he set to drying my hair in a methodical manner while his partner in crime stroked terrycloth over my body. I didn't question what had prompted this abrupt turn around, though I did feel bad that my lack had interrupted the first time that they—

"Stop that," Damien snapped.

"What?" I blinked at him.

"You don't *lack* anything, firecracker. And we're prepared to show you exactly that."

I wasn't tracking. Not when the two of them focused on drying themselves in a business-like way or when Damien plucked me up and carried me into the bedroom, with Mathis trailing behind. I shivered as my damp skin contacted cool, clean sheets.

"Lay back with your head hanging off the bed." Damien purred.

"Why?"

Mathis stroked my body leaving little electric tingles all along my skin. "We want to show you that you can take us deep. Or rather, take Damien." He looked up at the other shifter. "I'm already on the verge, so it'll have to be you."

Damien nodded as though it was a done deal and stood at the edge of the bed.

"Guys, I can't—" My words were cut off as Mathis pinched a nipple hard enough to make me cry out.

"You don't know until you try." Damien was sifting his claws through my hair again.

I shook my head. Didn't they get it?

"And what will happen if you can't?" Mathis growled. "You think either of us will love you any less?"

When I hesitated Damien added, "Sam, we know you have limitations. And that's okay. We can accept whatever you can give us. But we both feel like maybe you sometimes use the MS as an excuse because you're afraid to fail."

My teeth sank into my bottom lip. They weren't wrong.

Mathis smoothed his thumb across my lip, tugging it free. "This is supposed to be our fresh start. If you really can't do something, fine. We'll happily do something else. But to not even try to do something you want because you're worried about failing...you're better than that, love."

Nerves coursed through me but they were right. Whatever my limits were, I needed to know them. And the only way to do that was to step right up to the line. I laid back onto the mattress, scooting around until my head hung off the edge.

"Good, baby." Damien bent over me until he could suck my right nipple while Mathis tongued the left. Sharp erotic delight shimmered across my body. My lips parted and my skin felt flushed. I ached between my legs as the two of them sent me a slideshow of erotic images. Things we'd done. Things they'd wanted to try. With me and with each other.

Damien released my nipple with a wet pop. He

straightened and began stroking his claws along my throat. "Relax your jaw. I promise I'll go slow."

I swallowed and tried to obey. Mathis was working his way down my body, lapping at stray water droplets. When his calloused hands began stroking along my inner thighs, I gasped.

Damien aligned his shaft with my parted lips and urged my hand up to hold it in place. "Whenever you're ready, tug me forward, firecracker."

Blood was rushing to my head, but also to my sex . Mathis played around it, never touching too deeply, just enough to keep me hot, make me crave. Moisture beaded on the crown of Damien's penis and my tongue darted out to catch it. His legs quaked. My position made it obvious. I tugged him closer, opening so I could take him inside.

He groaned as he pushed past my lips. The head bumped along my tongue and the roof of my mouth. It felt weird with me being upside down, taking him this way, but not in a bad way. My lips covered my teeth so I wouldn't scrape sensitive flesh. When he hit the back of my throat my hand fell away. I dragged in air through my nose. My mouth had never felt so full.

He stilled, his muscles corded tight. "So good, Sam. So fucking good." Those claws were back on my throat, caressing me until I started to tingle all over.

Mathis began nuzzling my pubic hair. "Open up for me baby. You smell so hot and sweet. Let me lick you while you suck him."

A moan left me as I parted my thighs.

I swallowed and Damien gasped.

"Gods, Sam. I *felt* that everywhere."

"Then let's see if we can get her to do it again." Mathis shoved my legs farther apart and parted my labia with his thumbs so the cool late afternoon air caressed tender flesh. I shivered and Damien withdrew until only the head was still in my mouth. I whimpered in protest.

"Coming back, baby," he grated and then rolled his hips forward.

It went easier because I knew what to expect. Mathis lapped at my folds, making me moan around Damien's shaft.

"More?" He rasped when he hit the back of my throat again.

I couldn't speak but my eyes burned hot as he rocked back, then rolled forward, this time faster. I began pacing my breathing with his gentle movements, inhaling, and then sighing against him when he surged back in.

I forgot the awkwardness, the discomfort, all my fears. This was working. I was taking one of my lovers deep with my mouth.

His pace redoubled. I kept up, just barely. Mathis worked a finger into my body, fucking me in time with Damien's advances. I clenched around the digit and sank my nails into the backs of Damien's thighs, holding him steady while I swallowed and swallowed and swallowed.

He swore sharply. "Oh gods, oh gods, Sam, it's too good Can't choke you—"

He jerked out from between my lips and began coming across my naked chest and neck, using his hand to help wring the orgasm from him. I was short of breath and wide eyed, watching as his release went on and on and on. Just then Mathis sucked my clit between his lips and purred even while two of his fingers curled up inside me, finding that spot that made me....

Detonate.

I writhed under the onslaught of sensation, loving how sexually uninhibited I felt with one lover giving me a pearl necklace and the other licking up my orgasm. Damien looked as though he'd survived a bomb blast—barely. His blue eyes drank us in, Me, Mathis, and back up my semen-covered breast and belly.

When my second release finally subsided, I pushed Mathis's dark head away. "No more."

He growled at me, but he did stop. His lips shone with my gloss, eyes transfixed on the mess on my chest.

"You're gonna need another shower, little witch."

I groaned, this time from sheer exhaustion. "I'll make do with a washcloth."

No sooner were the words out of my mouth than Damien staggered into the bathroom. Through our bond I heard his thoughts. *I can't believe I just did that. That she wanted me to, that it made her come....*

Mathis gripped me by the hips and dragged me farther up onto the mattress before propping me up on the stack of pillows. He leaned over me, uncaring of the mess that could potentially glue us together. When we finally broke for air Damien stood beside the bed. still dumbstruck, wet washcloth in hand. Mathis grinned down at me. "You blew a lot more than his dick just now."

I preened and then quirked an eyebrow at Damien,

gesturing toward my chest. 'What, do I have to do everything?"

His lids lowered and he began wiping me clean. I settled back into the pillows, loving the petting, the murmurs of care and adoration that my mates heaped on me.

"Gods, Sam, your bond is pulsing with satisfaction," Damien whispered.

I caressed his whiskered cheek. "I'm feeling pleased with myself right now. Come here and kiss me."

He dropped the washcloth onto the floor and then surged up the bed. I took his mouth with mine, lapping my tongue against his.

A sharp slap made him jerk. Opening my eyes I spotted Mathis, still hard and eyeing Damien's backside intently.

In my arms Damien trembled. If not for the bond I would have guessed his reaction came from fear. Need made him quake. He wanted Mathis to take him, to fuck him. Badly. And he wanted me to hold him while he did it.

"On your back. Let her hold you. I need to see your face while I do this. Both of your faces." Mathis reached for the bedside drawer where we kept the lube. Squirting some into his palm he waited for Damien to comply.

I urged Damien to lay in my lap. His eyes had glazed over again as he stared up at my breasts, a claw poking at a nipple.

I stroked his hair. "You nervous?"

"A little." Didn't matter that I didn't possess a

shifter's sense of smell. With our three-way bond open, I could tell if he was being honest.

I stroked his hair and murmured. "Don't be. He's really very good at this."

Damien's hoarse exhalation turned into a groan as Mathis probed between his cheeks. He bucked and gasped when a slick finger worked inside him.

"Relax," Mathis's dark eyes were hot as he watched Damien squirm, then looked at me. "Sam's gonna think you can't take it."

I would think nothing of the sort. I saw how Damien's shaft was twitching, how his claw-tipped hands were shredding our sheets. Mathis wasn't just opening Damien up to fuck, I realized when he let out a ragged groan. "Are you massaging his prostate?

"Best orgasm a man can have." Mathis mumbled even as Damien let out a choked cry. When Mathis withdrew his fingers Damien muttered a protest, going so far to pull his knees up to his chest, splitting himself wide even as he nuzzled against my thigh as though seeking comfort.

I stroked his hair, in awe of how he looked at how all of this felt. Damien Moss, completely undone. I didn't know it was possible.

"You ready?" Mathis asked when he'd slicked his cock with lube He was so thick, so swollen, his balls heavy with seed. The only one who hadn't come yet.

Damien's nod was frantic. "Yes."

Mathis's got that evil twin look in his eye. "Beg me."

My mouth fell open. He didn't just say that!

Damien urged, "Please, please."

"Please what?" In a move designed to drive one mad Mathis fisted his shaft and pressed the plum shaped head against Damien's opening. Not hard enough to penetrate, just enough so that his partner could feel him there, ready to surge inside. To claim new territory.

Shifters and their games.

"Please Mathis, fuck me." Damien begged.

With victory shining in his eyes, Mathis shoved himself home with one hard plunge.

Damien's back bowed, his cock stood erect once more, his mouth hung open on a silent scream. He was poised on the razor's edge, stretched to his max around his lover's thick shaft, being filled and fucked and loved in a brand new way.

I petted his hair. "I'm so proud of you."

Mathis began to move on top of him, within him. He rolled his hips, stirring his cock, making Damien flail helplessly against him. The former alpha was totally undone by the sensations that swamped through his body. They buffeted against me like waves breaking against a cliff face.

"Harder," Damien pleaded too awash in sensation to worry about a little thing like pride.

Mathis drew back, his dark eyes on my face, assessing my reaction. I watched him with hot eyes as he drilled forward, shoving Damien farther up the mattress, into me. I winced as his head collided with my hipbone.

With a growl Mathis withdrew even as Damien shook his head. "What—"

"We'll hurt her that way. Turn over."

Scrambling to obey, Damien presented his backside

DIRECTRIX CUT SCENE

to Mathis. Then he caught sight of me curled up in my nest of pillows and some of the lust haze cleared. "You okay, Sam?"

"Maybe a bruise, no biggie." I gestured toward the reddened hip.

He prowled forward, his gaze on mine. "Forgive me?"

"Always," When I nodded he dropped a kiss to my hip, and then nuzzled at my groin.

"Let me make it up to you." He purred.

Mathis had already started easing back inside Damien. "I'll go easier," he vowed.

Trusting them completely, I spread my legs.

Damien's inhale was deep and long and resulted in a drawn-out purr. His tongue speared through my wetness and he groaned though there was no way to tell if it was from Mathis or me.

"Both," he thought down the bond. *"It's both of you."*

I leaned back, watching them move. Thick muscles bunching and coated with sweat as they worked to satisfy the mate they loved on. I drew closer and closer to the edge until,

Mathis gripped Damien by the hair and snarled, "Do you want to come inside her?"

When Damien nodded frantically, Mathis released him and looked to me, waiting.

I shifted down, so that Damien could reach me. He crawled over me and poised his cock at my wet opening. My sex clenched, needing to feel that shaft deep within me.

Mathis fucking Damien fucking me. It would be the Mac Daddy of all orgasms.

Damien rocked forward and seated himself to the base. Poised over me, inside me, he waited, blue eyes blazing with desire.

Gripping his hips, Mathis worked himself back into place. I felt the shove and cried out, my orgasm barreling over me. Damien groaned, "Gods, *Sam. Mathis.* So fucking good."

He jerked hard as I milked his shaft. The moment he finished shuddering, Mathis

wrapped an arm around Damien's neck, pulling him free. Dark brown and blue eyes focused on my spread sex. I slipped a finger down and worked my clit, greedy for another orgasm. Dual groans. Mathis sat back onto his haunches and he seated the other shifter on his plunging cock.

Our eyes met.

"Give him everything," I purred to Mathis as I masturbated harder, faster.

Mathis nodded and then thrust. Damien cried out again as Mathis bounced him hard, using the other man's deep orgasm to draw his own release. I saw it on both their faces, felt it through both bonds. Damien's body jerked as though electrified, twitching hard. As though he hadn't just orgasmed. Mathis fucked him hard and deep and finally came with a primal roar of victory.

We were all sticky, flushed and panting by the time the final spasms abated. Hearts thundering, we settled down to catch our breath. Damien nuzzled my neck and fell into an exhausted sleep. Mathis cupped one of my breasts in his big palms.

"Cold?" He asked when I shivered.

I shook my head. "Sensitized."

"Have I said thank you, yet?" he asked quietly.

"For what?" I whispered.

"For being you, little witch." He offered me a contented smile. "Your trust, your acceptance, your love...it's more than I'd ever hoped to find."

And through our newly forged connection, I felt an even deeper thread that pulsed like a heartbeat.

"What's that?" I whispered as I flashed the image back to him.

His lips curled. "That my love, is our mating bond."

A sigh escaped. Everything was right in our little corner of the world.

Made in the USA
Columbia, SC
21 July 2023